MW00526764

"In Roger's Thought-Particles Joram ̶̶̶̶̶̶̶, a ̶̶̶̶ ̶̶̶̶ ̶̶̶̶̶̶̶̶, moves seamlessly between the real and the imagined. Roger, a young research scientist with an over-sized ego, consults regularly with the "living hallucination" of his great-great-grandfather, Ricardo—whose struggles to gain recognition for some over-the-edge research "findings" mirror Roger's own. A mysterious "Virerium" pandemic that seemingly transmits personality trait-bearing thought-particles from the brains of one person to another may give Roger a breakthrough opportunity. He thinks the knows the source, an "imagination gene." Will Roger finally gain the recognition he craves? Is this science or fiction? Reading this novel is a fun, suspenseful adventure."

—Douglas Alan Walrath,
Author of *The Daredancers*

"Joram Piatigorsky's novel, Roger's Thought Particles, melds storytelling and philosophy in a single work. The protagonist, Dr. Roger Resin, and his alter-ego, his deceased great-great-grandfather Ricardo Sztein, debate the nature of thought, imagination, and science as Roger develops a controversial and potentially ground-breaking theory that, if true, could change the way people view the world. As Roger's theory takes shape, we're introduced to a colorful cast of characters, some of whom are changed by Roger's grand conjecture, and others who are catalysts for Roger's own metamorphosis."

—Lewis J. Beilman III,
Author of *The Changing Tide*

"Humility wasn't one of Roger's traits," writes author Joram Piatigorsky in his captivating new novel, Roger's Thought Particles. And we hold on to our hats as Dr. Roger Resin, a respected and award-winning scientist, arrogantly barges his way through the halls of the Vision Science Center on a quest to find a way to associate belief and optimism within the rigorous discipline of the scientific method. A lively cast of characters, including his spectral great-great-grandfather, Ricardo, join Roger, sometimes helping, but often throwing practical advice in the way of his fanciful dream. Can Roger resist his well-meaning friends' concerns and fulfill his unconventional pursuit? You'll be surprised when Piatigorsky's imaginative ending sends Roger off on a whole new tangent in which belief comes to terms with rational thought."

—James White,
Author of *Borders in Paradise*
and *Ransoms Are for Amateurs*

"Joram Piatigorsky has mastered one of science's most intriguing topics: telepathy. In his new novel Roger's Thought Particles, Piatigorsky explores one man's devotion to science and his ambitious intent to prove that thoughts are not simply transferred by word of mouth, but by infectious thought particles. Piatigorsky not only grasps the language of science, he presents a compelling look inside the mind, leaving readers to ponder whether thoughts are our own or transferred from one another by simply being in the same room."

—Tara Lynn Marta,
Author of *Look Back to Yesterday*
and *Dreaming Through the Eyes of God*

Roger Resin has wanted to make his mark on the world of science ever since he was a biology major at Yale…While Roger spends his days pursuing what he calls "the useful mundane" - practical science related to improving health - he daydreams about bigger mysteries, like the source of imagination… How do genes, or how does chemistry, or whatever, create imagination?"…Piatigorsky's prose is measured and clear, deftly satirizing certain real-world trends (including a mysterious pandemic that strikes when Roger is middle-aged)…the book grapples with captivating themes like the weight of influence, the validity of unorthodox research, and the frontiers where biology and imagination meet. An intriguing…ideas-driven tale of a haunted scientist.

—*Kirkus Reviews*

If you have wondered about the thoughts and goals of a research scientist, read this novel by the distinguished scientist/ author, Joram Piatigorsky. Roger's journey through a life of science will give you the insight you seek. His interactions with colleagues, both real and imagined, the challenges of research and the tribulations that accompany it, are all revealed. But that is before the story expands dramatically with the pandemic, the idea of Thought-Particles, and the redirection of Roger's life.

—Robert Wurtz,
NIH Scientist Emeritus,
member National Academy of Sciences U.S.A.

Roger's Thought-Particles enters no-man's land on the frontier between imagination and science. There's nobody better suited to probe this terrain than scientist Joram Piatigorsky.

—Roger Herst,
Author of *The Rabbi Gabrielle Series*.

"A thoughtful novel about the nature of thinking, *Roger's Thought-Particles* is by turns philosophical, speculative, and even madcap. Most of all, it's a pleasure to read from start to finish."

—Zach Powers,
Author of *First Cosmic Velocity*

"In the current era of contagions, pandemics, and the melding of science and suspicions, the living hallucinations and thought particles in this imaginative and colorful work will infect readers with possibility, optimism and creative alternatives to the concept of reality and inoculate against boredom!"

—Ronda Beaman,
Founder and Executive Director, Dream Makers SLO,
Clinical Professor, Orfalea College of Business, and
Author of *My Feats in These Shoes*,
Little Miss Merit Badge, and *You're Only Young Twice*

ROGER'S THOUGHT-PARTICLES

Roger's Thought-Particles

A novel

by

JORAM PIATIGORSKY

Adelaide Books
New York / Lisbon
2021

ROGER'S THOUGHT-PARTICLES
A novel
By Joram Piatigorsky

Copyright © by Joram Piatigorsky
Cover design © 2021 Adelaide Books

Published by Adelaide Books, New York / Lisbon
adelaidebooks.org

Editor-in-Chief
Stevan V. Nikolic

All rights reserved. No part of this book may be reproduced in any manner whatsoever without written permission from the author except in the case of brief quotations embodied in critical articles and reviews.

For any information, please address Adelaide Books
at info@adelaidebooks.org
or write to:
Adelaide Books
244 Fifth Ave. Suite D27
New York, NY, 10001

ISBN: 978-1-955196-68-0

Printed in the United States of America

To Ricardo Sztein (1977 – 2059)

Founder, Scientist, Dreamer

"...I knew that my dreams had been right a thousand times over...It was life and reality that were wrong."

"...for in the last resort they have to share their beliefs in order to live."

Hermann Hesse, *Steppenwolfe*

Contents

PART II: THE PANDEMIC

PART III: THINKING

PART IV: THOUGHT-PARTICLES

PART V: PUBLICATION

Prologue

Roger, somewhat agitated, continued splashing around in his muddled thoughts about thinking. His wife, Robin, sighed and checked her wristwatch. 10:30 already, and her dental appointment was at 11:00. Obsessive about being punctual, time for her had a hard reality.

"I know it doesn't make much sense, Robin, but still, honestly, thoughts come from somewhere, and…listen to this…"

She looked annoyed.

But Roger was virtually bursting to tell Robin his latest ideas about thoughts and their passing from one person to another. Before him, no one had even considered transforming abstract thoughts into particles. He wanted to bring her up to date – now – on the latest progress of his revolutionary insight. She had smarts, the ability to see things as they were, not as they might be by imposing her own ideas. She didn't bend reality. He wanted her opinion – needed it – and to be truthful, he wanted her praise. His new concept was clever and beautiful, that was his opinion. It was still speculative, of course, like all new hypotheses, but he believed he was right – he had the data. It made sense and had widespread implications.

Robin always listened patiently to his monologues, which occurred with growing frequency as he sank deeper and deeper into his research on thought. He was determined to succeed this time. It was the best idea he ever had, and he desperately wanted it to repair his dwindling reputation after he had made a big deal of announcing the discovery of a nonexistent gene responsible for imagination. It was ironic that his greatest asset – a remarkable imagination – turned out to be his most vulnerable trait.

Robin had a magical gift to understand and support him, not by fanfare, but by listening and keeping his imagination in check. He depended on her as a silent accomplice for emotional stability.

"Please, Roger, I have to be at the dentist in thirty minutes. I've got to go now. Sorry."

"Sure, fine. One more thing though," Roger persisted. "Remember…"

Robin forced a smile. As much as she loved Roger, she admitted he could be overly persistent, and stubborn, very stubborn, although he was bright and devoted to science. She admired his roaming and inclusive mind, and the courage he had to risk crossing the borders of science. Robin did her best not to lose patience when he drifted from science to fantasy.

"Let's continue tonight, Roger. All right?" She eyed the front door.

After Robin left for her dental appointment, Roger went into his dimly lit study lined with shelves stuffed with books on a wide range of topics – science, fiction, biography, poetry – on one side of the room, and messy stacks of science and literary journals on the other side. Five antique wooden African staffs, beautiful prestige symbols of tribal chiefs from the early 20th century, stood in a corner, rare items for the mid-22nd century. His desk, littered with manuscripts and extraneous papers, was situated a small distance in front of the bookshelves. An Inuit sculpture of a kneeling caribou rested next to his computer on the desk. In Roger's opinion, the ethnic and tribal arts complemented the creative nature of his basic research in science, which he viewed as the foundation for the portrait of life. Art and science merged in Roger's mind, as if they belonged together, each reinforcing the other.

Roger's favorite chair, covered by a worn leather upholstery with a dark, aged patina, was firmly implanted by the desk. The chair was a family heirloom from Ricardo Sztein, his Argentinean great-great-grandfather, who had immigrated to the United States late in the 20th century as a graduate student and became a scientist, like Roger.

Overcome by a wave of fatigue, Roger sank into the armchair, closed his eyes, and let his mind drift. Although relaxed at first, anxiety stole the peace as his thoughts turned to the pressure he felt from his Scientific Director and peers to focus his research on immediate medical problems; this, in turn, triggered his frustration about how often the honors went to medical advances rather than to basic discoveries with no known application yet. Roger felt trapped in a moral prison of social obligations for his research. Yet, he loved the science, which constrained him in his imaginary jail cell.

At such moments of conflict, Ricardo appeared in his thoughts. Yes, Ricardo was dead – true enough – he had died long ago – but never mind the five generations of separation between the two scientists. Ricardo lived in Roger's life, and Roger kept a foothold in Ricardo's past. Time was a curious medium for Roger, who allowed all the players – past and present – to interact in a continuous whirlwind.

As if by magic, Roger sensed Ricardo's presence and sat upright, and there stood his distant kin.

"Hello," Ricardo greeted Roger with a friendly wave of his left hand. Ricardo was left-handed, as was Roger.

"Hi, Ricardo. Good to see you."

Smiling and pudgy as always, Ricardo looked in good health, and his eyes burned with intensity. His attire projected his idiosyncrasies: wrinkled pants with a rope for a belt, a brown corduroy sports jacket with coffee stains, a striped shirt unbuttoned at the neck, and scuffed shoes, with the sole of one needing repair. He was wearing unmatched socks, one red with white dots, the other green, a color catastrophe. He looked... well...like Ricardo, more alive than an apparition.

"What brings you here now, Ricardo? Is this a social visit, or what?"

Roger didn't need to ask that since he knew. Ricardo wore unmatched socks when it was a social visit or when Roger invited him for company. If Ricardo appeared during a crisis or special occasion, he wore matching bright orange socks, which he said was appropriate for consequential events. The color attracted attention, like a warning of sorts, and orange was the only word in the English language that didn't rhyme with any other word. Orange stood out and was unique, like important events.

"I haven't spoken to you for some time," said Ricardo, "and I was excited to hear your new ideas about thoughts. Pretty ingenious. Good for you..."

Ricardo had a direct line to Roger's life and thoughts, as if his brain and consciousness were tethered to Roger's. Ricardo always knew what was in Roger's mind, so Roger couldn't keep any secrets from him. This was not reciprocal, however. Roger only knew what Ricardo chose to tell him. All relationships have their inequality.

Robin's voice from the kitchen interrupted Ricardo. "Want some lunch, Roger? I brought a pizza home."

Roger looked at his watch – 12:15.

"Back already, Robin? That was quick," he answered. "Sure, pizza sounds good. I'll be right there."

"Were you talking to someone?" she called back from the kitchen. "It sounded like there was someone with you?"

"No. I was just mumbling to myself."

Robin knew about Roger's preoccupation with Ricardo and that he admired his courage to have bucked the political system. When Roger had told her that he wished he could do the same as Ricardo – go out on a limb and do some truly innovative work looking for hidden gems of nature – she reminded him of Ricardo's fate. Did he, Roger, really want to end in jail, or be fired, or who knows what else? Of course not, he had said. However, she had no inkling how close the two scientists were, and how much that meant to Roger. Roger kept it that way, partly out of embarrassment, and partly because he respected Ricardo's private life, for he too must have had his reasons for becoming part of Roger's private life.

Their story, then, is a fairy tale, the kind that can never be proved, yet flourishes in belief.

PART I

ROGER AND RICARDO

First Encounter

Humility wasn't one of Roger's traits. He was ambitious beyond his years and daydreamed of making extraordinary achievements already as an undergraduate at Yale majoring in biology. He was frustrated being a lowly student for so many years. Perhaps because his mother, an actor, spent her life impersonating characters invented by playwrights, Roger rebelled against being guided by anyone else's creative endeavors. He wanted to be creative himself, and thus he followed his own independent course in college, often skipping classes to read whatever interested him rather than do his assignments. His goal was to do just enough to get by.

Of his readings, *Jellyfish Have Eyes* had the greatest impact on him. That historical biography elevated Ricardo Sztein, who became Roger's alter ego, from an abstract family name of a distant relative to a "living" person.

Roger's appreciation of Ricardo, the adventurous scientist, started when he realized how important and creative it was to think beyond conventional beliefs. Ricardo's experiments indicating that jellyfish visualized evolution hooked him, although he struggled with the fact that Ricardo ended his life in prison, convicted of squandering government funds for irrelevant research. He called Ricardo's imagination and independence "busting the barrier of confinement," and he thought his conviction grossly unfair. This understandably created for Roger a conflict of great admiration mingled with concern. Nonetheless, Roger wondered whether he would ever come up with such a creative, paradigm-shifting hypothesis himself, as Ricardo did. While his classmates at Yale, except for his best friend, Nathan, discussed what they had learned in class and how to prepare for exams, Roger conversed incessantly with Ricardo, sought his opinion about matters from trivial to vital, and confided his aspirations to him. He debated with Ricardo at length about whether invertebrates may in some ways be more advanced creatures than humans, and Ricardo convinced him that these ancient animals lacking a backbone had a lot to teach humans.

In brief, Ricardo presented a progressive world of imagination and innovation, yet tainted with danger. Despite his close bond with Ricardo, Roger continued to harbor a deep worry – bordering on fear – that he too might end as a felon by being too independent, as Ricardo was, to the point of apparent arrogance.

What Roger didn't appreciate then or later was that Ricardo was as devoted to Roger as Roger was obsessed with him. How could Roger have been aware of Ricardo's buried motivation? But it must have been true to some extent – perhaps not even clearly in Ricardo's mind – that Roger might give him another chance, at least vicariously, to realize his own dreams to overcome his humiliating legacy.

But friends they were, deeply attached and committed to each other. Ricardo came when Roger summoned him, as well as often on his own initiative. How much Roger appreciated his relationship with Ricardo, and how much security and confidence Ricardo gave him!

Ricardo had inhabited the "wilderness of ignorance," as he called it, where his curiosity and imagination merged when he investigated jellyfish vision in the mangrove swamp of Puerto Rico. Roger too wanted to dance to his own tune by following his insatiable curiosity of the natural world, and he set his goals as a scientist, as premature as that was, sky high in the clouds.

In short, Roger wished he could be like Ricardo. But towering goals risked failure and gnawed at Roger. He imagined himself standing on the edge of a cliff overlooking the ocean, a gift to behold, enticing him to jump into the endless expanse and join the mysterious miracles beneath the surface. Taking that leap was almost irresistible. But there were sharp boulders on the ground, which meant certain death if he didn't avoid them by jumping far enough forward. Ricardo had taken that metaphorical risk when he used precious government funds, at a time of a pervading economic depression, and published his research suggesting the incredulous and unprovable notion that jellyfish had a brain and could visualize evolution. Oh, the boldness, the imagination, the freedom of such research! Ricardo was a hero in Roger's mind, but, sadly, not in the eyes of Ricardo's troubled era. If Ricardo was a hero, he was an unsung hero. He was tried and convicted for his research deemed to be irrelevant and a waste of taxpayers' money.

Poor conflicted Roger, who dreamed about freedom to explore new vistas, such as Ricardo did, while at the same time feared Ricardo's devastating and unfair fate.

The Cart Before the Horse

Consistent with his cavalier attitude, Roger considered rote academic exercises at Yale in his science courses a waste of time that could be used trying to solve problems that remained unanswered. How foolish, how immature that was, as the teaching assistant (TA) in Roger's organic chemistry course tried unsuccessfully to let him know.

"Can't you just tell me how to synthesize that steroid instead of my spending half the weekend trying to figure it out? You and others already know how to do it. Since when has re-inventing the wheel been a good use of time?"

Roger was incurably impatient.

"Roger, be reasonable," said the TA brusquely, seemingly anxious to get back to his work. "How do you expect to learn anything if someone else has to tell you how to solve these problems?"

Roger dodged the question and said, "If you tell me the answer, I'll know it and then be able to work on problems that no one has solved. That would be much more stimulating and productive. I want to have some impact in my short time on this."

Roger's suggestion that he had only a short time on planet Earth was nonsense for dramatic effect. The TA must have understood that. But Roger wanting to have impact before Mother Nature removes him from Earth…that was true.

Ricardo, uninvited, appeared suddenly sitting on a stool.

"Re-inventing the wheel, Roger? Aren't you going a bit too far? The TA is only doing his job," said Ricardo. "Do you really want to have success handed to you on a silver platter with no effort on your part?"

Roger was taken aback for a moment by his friend and defender not supporting him. No, he didn't want undeserved success. He never wanted anything he didn't earn. Before he had time to tell that to Ricardo, the TA broke the silence.

"That's ridiculous," said the TA. "You're young and have to learn how to do things yourself. The specific answer to any exercise is irrelevant. It's learning *how* to solve such problems that matters."

Roger didn't buy it, and he looked for Ricardo to agree with him. A simple nod would have been enough, but no such luck. Ricardo wasn't there anymore. How annoying! Ricardo came when called – great – and sometimes he appeared when he felt needed or interested or to socialize – fine. However, he always left, vaporized into thin air, whenever he wanted. Roger had no control of that, so he never knew whether Ricardo was bored or angry or testing Roger's ability to fend for himself, which he had to do now.

"What about mirror neurons?" Roger asked.

"What?" The TA raised his eyebrows.

Ricardo came back to the scene, seated on the stool again, looking confident.

"Good going, Roger. Support your argument, even if, I must say, it's strange. Never mind. Far-out ideas need scientific support and then, who knows? You may even convince some people. Keep that in mind. Science first, then go for it."

Roger regained his confidence with Ricardo back.

"Mirror neurons, the neurons that are responsible for mimicking some feelings of others in sight. Mirror neurons in the brain fire to mimic what's being observed. Don't you feel like crying when you see someone else cry? Mirror neurons cause feeling by mimicking behavior. If feelings can be transferred passively, why can't the same be true for information?

"Look," Roger continued, "learning by imitation is nature's way. Even an octopus can learn by watching another octopus. I'm not kidding. I read about an octopus alone in an aquarium struggling for some time to unscrew the top of a bottle that contains food, while another octopus watched in the adjacent aquarium. Once the first octopus succeeded, the voyeur octopus was given the same capped bottle with food in it and opened it quickly. He learned how to unscrew the bottle and get the food simply by watching! That's what I mean. Show me, and then I'll know it too."

Roger looked satisfied, and then went on, lacking good judgment on when to stop. "I've learned just about everything I know by being told or by reading," he said, "not by writing the book. The authors *tell* me their ideas; they don't ask anything from me. I'm a sponge that soaks up knowledge that I can use when I need or want to. Isn't that learning by being told?"

Roger twisted things in his favor, even when he appeared to contradict himself. For example, he praised reading to absorb knowledge passively, but then he added, "But reading isn't sufficient, since whatever is written in a book is someone else's idea." That created a conundrum – learn by reading, but don't spend time on the author's ideas. He rescued the apparent contradiction between reading to learn, yet resenting the time spent on the ideas of others, by saying, "Read to learn what is not yet written."

Ricardo looked stern.

"Careful, Roger. Don't pull the rug out from under yourself with sophistry. My ideas on jellyfish were original, that's for sure, but not because I wanted to be different or novel. Imagination doesn't mean rebellion; imagination isn't a weapon or ladder to climb for success. Not every idea needs to be overturned. I didn't speculate that jellyfish had a type of brain or could visualize evolution because no one thought they did or to make myself famous. Got it!"

Roger craved to be like Ricardo – his hero – who wrote his own story, his creation, blending the lofty position of man with the low status of jellyfish. But he wasn't convinced that Ricardo was so selfless. Dead people were less accountable.

Ricardo, certainly not appearing dead, said as if he read Roger's mind, "Come on, Roger. You can't tread in my past path, follow my footsteps, and make your own footprints at the same time. You've got to choose between being a *follower* or a *leader*."

Roger, knowing that Ricardo had a point, said to himself, "I know that! Just because you inspire me doesn't mean I want to follow you to jail."

Wishing that Ricardo would disappear again, yet stubborn as usual, Roger wasn't going to let his idol defeat him. No sir! He wasn't through arguing with the TA either.

"What about computers?" he asked, stretching for more scientific support in his favor. "They manipulate downloaded data and come up with new findings. Aren't our brains also computers that benefit from receiving information passively – isn't that what downloading is all about? Don't we too, like computers, spit out what's new by digesting what we've been fed, by manipulating what's already known?"

The TA responded, "Maybe you should be a literature or, better yet, a philosophy major."

With that, Ricardo disappeared. He had no interest in literature or philosophy.

Roger thanked the TA, left, and never bothered to solve the assigned problem that he had gone to see him about. (Actually, he told a friend that he tried but gave up when he couldn't solve it.)

Boredom

Roger graduated from Yale with a biochemistry degree – cum laude, remarkably – and went for a PhD at the University of California at Berkeley in the laboratory of Dr. Paul Sash, an assistant professor skyrocketing to stardom in the field of molecular biology. Roger picked him as a mentor because of his intelligence, ambition, and youth, hoping that he would be thinking boldly and imaginatively about the future rather than being stuck in the past trudging on long-term projects that took forever to go nowhere. That didn't work out as expected.

Paul, who preferred to be called Dr. Sash, focused on "flavors-of-the-day," as Roger called them, namely, projects that attracted attention, the so-called current bandwagons. Once, when Roger told him about Ricardo at a social occasion, Dr. Sash said, "What did the guy expect from his off-beat research? Jail may have been extreme, but why would anyone care about what a jellyfish might or might not see, especially when there's no way to know if his wild ideas are right? Maybe if Ricardo had tried to find a soothing balm to jellyfish stings, it would have been different. He sounds like a martyr to me. Do you give birthday presents that you may like but are pretty sure that the recipients wouldn't care about at all? Of course not. We're social creatures, we try to fit in, satisfy what others want or need. Do you think grocery stores would survive selling hay for food? Well, maybe some sales would be made to people who have horses."

Paul – Dr. Sash – and Roger didn't become close friends.

Roger's PhD research project was to crystallize a protein that might – it wasn't certain – play a role in macular degeneration, a much feared and major cause of age-related blindness. This pathology received much attention by physicians, politicians and, especially, funding sources. Different students in Dr. Sash's laboratory had similar projects focusing on a variety of pathologies. They called themselves "the disease scouts." While Roger was a successful graduate student and published four articles in medical journals, he felt more in an assembly line than on the forefront of science, although he admitted that the severity of macular degeneration justified the funding of his research, and it would be quite something if his research findings eventually helped patients.

"Don't be arrogant, Roger," said Ricardo, when Roger complained about his research, even after he had articles accepted for publication in prestigious journals. "Maybe Dr. Sash has a point: if I had spent more time doing research to treat disease instead of what jellyfish see, I would have been praised, not vilified. At least I wouldn't have been put behind bars. Well... I don't know. Maybe...maybe not...who knows? You are who you are, no? Skin is the bars of the greatest prison of all. Oneself."

Roger worked diligently on his research and discussed endlessly with Ricardo on diverse esoteric topics, such as the risk of independent thinking, what it means to be true to oneself, and the like. The most stimulating questions for Roger that they debated were how does one think and how did thinking evolve?

Ricardo seemed to benefit from these discussions as much as, if not more than, Roger. Perhaps he just had more time to think, while Roger was buried in his research to finish his PhD thesis. Ricardo also seemed as engaged in the future as Roger, as if he had a dog in this struggle for achievement.

"These topics we discuss are fascinating, but hardly science, wouldn't you say?" Ricardo wondered one lazy Sunday afternoon when Roger decided to take the day off work. "Do you think questions with ambiguous answers can be considered scientific questions? Unless it's possible to prove or disprove something, I don't think it's a part of science. I don't know if I ever thought about that before. Thanks, Roger. I'm learning a lot from you."

Since Roger's tendency was to find a counterargument to everything, often an annoying trait, he said, "Maybe, Ricardo, but what do think about names?"

"Names? That's not a question, Roger."

"You may be partly right, but there's no way to know to what extent a name is correct or the best choice for calling any-thing. Yet, science couldn't exist without naming everything. Every protein and compound and species must have a name – everything is called something to identify it and keep order – but no name is definitive, and it always excludes some vital aspect. In other words, there isn't just one perfect name for something. It's only selectively correct. If the name is helpful, okay. Take a protein, for example. It can be called by its function, or by its lack of function if mutated, or by its structure, or by its location, or by its discoverer – on and on and on. No protein has a name that covers all its properties. Hemoglobin is about oxygen trans-port, right? Crystallins are the major proteins in the crystal-clear lens. Fine. But hemoglobin does far more than just transport oxygen, and crystallins do all kinds of different jobs in different tissues. Names of proteins, or of anything, are never inclusive. How much do you know about a protein by its name? Just a bit, I'd say. Names can be ambiguous, so are they part of science?"

"Of course. Are you kidding? Don't try to trick me," Ricardo answered. "What do *you* think?"

"That I'm bored with my research on the structure of a single protein that may or may not be important for macular degeneration."

That was enough for Ricardo to disappear, as quickly as fingers snap. He didn't like to take part in self-indulgent blabber. He found *that* boring.

Concurrent with receiving his doctorate, Roger reaped the benefits of his medically relevant publications on macular degeneration. The Vision Science Center in Washington, seeking new young scientists, invited him for an interview and to present a lecture on his research. Two weeks later, they offered him the opportunity to start a laboratory in their august institution.

Too good to be true, Roger dispensed with a postdoctoral fellowship, the common pathway of new PhDs, accepted the offer, moved to Washington and set out to conquer the world of science.

The 'Imagination' Gene

Ricardo was ecstatic when Roger told him that he was going to start a laboratory at the Vision Science Center, the very same institution that had employed him.

"It's like reliving my life," Ricardo said, his voice trembling in excitement. "Thank you. Thank you. I can't wait until you start working there. I'm so happy. Be bold! I'm with you. We're together. We'll be a great success!"

"*Together*? *We'll* be a great success?" Roger muttered quietly to himself.

What was Ricardo thinking? Roger had been offered the opportunity to start a laboratory, not Ricardo. Ricardo had had his chance. Was Ricardo blurring the line between their separate identities? Perhaps, but then again, it seemed that Ricardo was an integral part of Roger. In any case, Ricardo was Roger's closest friend and mentor and confidant. No matter what Ricardo thought, this wasn't his career. It was Roger's, wasn't it?

Since Roger needed to be productive as quickly as possible to obtain tenure, he continued along the successful research path he had as a graduate student. He labored intensively investigating patterns of expression of different proteins that might have a role in various eye diseases. The research was short on innovation but long on applications involved in protein isolation and gene analysis. Roger attracted many freshly minted postdoctoral fellows, of whom most were research-oriented physicians. His laboratory published many research reports, and he reviewed articles for journals and grants for funding and gave invited lectures at academic institutions and scientific conferences. By all the usual criteria, he was a rising star in his field. Yet, he often felt like a battery-operated machine.

Ricardo continued to pop up now and then, however less frequently as time passed, and always with non-matching socks. There was nothing pressing or of immediate concern. He occasionally yawned during these visits, which Roger had not noted before.

"Tired, Ricardo?" Roger once asked.

"Not really," he answered. "But, you know, the days seem longer than usual, I guess. Any plans for some adventures?"

Roger, not prepared for the question, didn't answer. Adventures? Did he have any plans? Wasn't he too busy for that? Macular degeneration – losing vision – was terrifying. He had enough on his plate. But still, although macular degeneration was a major medical issue...yes...but it was new concepts he cared about. He missed not having adventures, as Ricardo put it. He had a point. Had he planted a seed in Roger's mind?

Roger's reputation grew as he labored, yet he remained restless and unsatisfied. He thought his research findings amounted to small discoveries, although some had bigger possibilities, if they worked out, that is, which was rarely, and so forth. Every research article ended with "more research is warranted." Was that progress? It was like saying "live longer to salvage deficiencies." Nothing was conceptually new. As important as solving problems was, he wasn't opening new vistas to explore.

When his friend Nathan, who remained closely in touch with Roger since college, asked him why he seemed disgruntled so often, Roger typically said, "Because I want to swim in an ocean, not wade in a stream."

"Really? What do you mean?"

"I'm bored, Nathan. I want to do something new, innovative. I'm tired of fiddling with details. I want to broaden perspectives. I want adventure – granted, intellectual adventure – but nonetheless adventure, to find a gem in the 'wilderness of ignorance,' as Ricardo called it when he bucked the system and investigated jellyfish. *That* was an adventure!"

The moment Roger said those words, he visualized a jail cell with thick bars. He expected Ricardo to make a quick entrance, but he didn't. Instead, he said softly in Roger's mind, "I know what you mean, Roger, and you're right, the wilderness of ignorance is exciting and challenging, but be prepared for the unexpected. The surprises can be different than anything you imagined. It's never what you think it might be."

Ricardo could be inconsistent and confusing. Positive one day, cautious the next. What happened to him since he was so excited about Roger's new job at the Vision Science Center? Why the dour outlook now? Was he suddenly afraid that he really had become Roger, had become reincarnated, like he had insinuated? If so, would that heap more failure on him? Or was he trying to be a helpful mentor, an experienced friend and protector? Well, thought Roger, did any one of these possibilities exclude any of the others? Was there a limit to the number of dimensions that existed in life, or types of ghosts that resided in a person?

While the postdoctoral fellows labored on what Roger considered "the useful mundane," he read science fiction stories and fantasy tales about far away planets with life forms that have never been seen. One day when he was pondering Pablo

Picasso's statement, "Everything you can imagine is real," Ricardo appeared, this time wearing matching orange socks. He bounced with enthusiasm.

"Yes! That's it, Roger," he said. "What you can imagine can become real. I believe that. Where do you think imagination comes from? Outer space? An empty barrel? A squirrel? No! I'm being silly. I know. Imagination comes from brains, a living tissue, and it must be defined by our genes – human genes – yours and mine! How does that work? How do genes, or how does chemistry, or whatever, create imagination?"

Oh, he was so excited. It was the Ricardo from his biography, and the Ricardo when Roger accepted the job at the Vision Science Center, the Ricardo that Roger loved and admired. Yes, imagination was real, and it must have a genetic root. He would hunt for an Imagination gene.

Roger started comparing myriad genetic sequences searching for any that are strictly in humans and possibly a candidate for the ability to imagine. Ricardo watched from a distance, interested, especially since he had inspired the idea, but he thought Roger's approach and leap of assumptions, one over another, on and on, were a waste of time. He finally felt he should let Roger know this in strong terms. But Roger didn't care anymore what Ricardo thought.

"It's risky, but an amazing idea, Ricardo, a completely new concept. It's not solving a problem, it's discovering phenomena," Roger said. "Have faith, Ricardo. I thought you wanted me to be bold. Linking a gene to imagination would be as revolutionary as was linking DNA sequences to life. What a bombshell that was! This is a step in that direction. Erwin Schrödinger asked, *What is Life?* I'll ask, *What is Imagination?*"

There was no stopping Roger on this mad pursuit. He finally settled on a relatively short DNA fragment that was present uniquely in human DNA. And then Roger did something extraordinary that impressed even Ricardo. Somehow, and Ricardo couldn't figure out how he did it, Roger convinced especially creative and imaginative individuals – Nobel Prize winners, writers, artists, business tycoons – to contribute DNA samples that he could search for the potential sequence for an "Imagination" gene.

Ricardo stayed relatively silent during this period, which took over a year. There was nothing he could do or say that would discourage Roger, and Roger hoped that Ricardo's absence meant that he was intensely interested and waiting for the findings.

Roger's data! Oh, my god! Incredible! The sequence, which he called the potential "Imagination" gene, was not only present in every sample from his collection of creative individuals, but it was amplified ten or more times over the control samples, namely, DNA of the so-called ordinary persons, not so intellectually gifted.

"Isn't it amazing, Ricardo?" Roger asked as he was writing a draft of his groundbreaking "Imagination" gene for publication. "This is truly new."

"Yeah, interesting, I admit that, although somewhat biased and prejudiced, I'd say. Are you implying that the 'ordinary' people are less smart in some way? Come on, Roger. Linking genetics to intelligence of any kind…I don't know. It's so speculative, and snobbish to some extent. I wouldn't be surprised if your interpretation of this enriched sequence is only imaginative, and certainly not a gene for imagination. Do you even have any idea what imagination is? I mean, how is it different from any other thought? Can imagination be confined to a gene? I'd be careful if I were you."

Roger was disappointed with Ricardo's negative reaction, but at least he had made the distinction between himself and

Roger. That made the "Imagination" gene truly his and his alone. Ricardo wasn't talking about Roger's work as his too.

After several submissions to different journals, a relatively minor psychiatry journal accepted the article, much to Ricardo's surprise, but the journal included an editorial upfront saying that the imaginative article was meant to illustrate how little was still known about the mind and the need to be open-minded to make progress in understanding the brain. Kudos to Dr. Roger Resin for such imagination!

Ricardo was surprised that the editors would resort to such sarcasm, and it wasn't "kudos" that Roger received. The article was ridiculed by psychiatrists, and then dispensed with by geneticists when the same sequence was found in several rare species of insects, a tropical fish, and a host of viruses. The consensus opinion was that Roger's "Imagination" gene was imaginative. Period. There was speculation that the sequence was a remnant of inserted viral DNA from long ago, or possibly it was an arbitrary fragment of DNA for some non-essential function. That it was amplified in Roger's "imaginative" sample was certainly a fluke. Who knows? The functions of most DNA remained mysterious. The journal would have done Roger a favor by rejecting the article, as the other journals did.

Roger was despondent. Ricardo tried everything to be uplifting but without success. Roger promised himself if he could live this down, he would never again let his imagination get the better of him. He promised himself he would tame his ambition.

But could Roger ever lower his ambition? Ricardo doubted it and took Roger's promise like Mark Twain's that "giving up smoking is the easiest thing in the world. I know because I've done it thousands of times."

But, as Ricardo's life had shown, fate is happenstance. It wasn't a promise to himself that rescued Roger from the pit of defeat, it was Robin.

Robin

Roger moped, felt crushed and humiliated. He wondered how he could recover from having made a fool of himself. Perhaps he should quit science and find another, safer career. However, after a few weeks he wrote a retraction to his innovative "Imagination" gene, admitting he had overinterpreted the data, but still, he said, "the potential to imagine remains a fascinating issue worthy of further consideration."

This didn't sound like he was about to quit science.

During this dark year, Roger retreated into himself, spent most of the time in the laboratory doing mostly mechanical chores. He did not socialize, and he wallowed in self-pity. When he envisioned a bleak future, Ricardo appeared and told him he was still young, his life was before him. It didn't do much to elevate Roger's mood.

One evening Roger stayed in the laboratory longer than usual and Ricardo dashed in for a rendezvous, as he called it, which Roger found a bit pompous and not quite accurate. A rendezvous wasn't spontaneous; it was an arranged meeting, which Ricardo never made. Ricardo was especially chatty that evening.

"Is this what you want – to be miserable forever?" Ricardo asked.

"Shut up, Ricardo," Roger snapped back. "I'm not miserable," he lied.

"No, I won't shut up. That's not what you really want anyway, is it? When are you going to rejoin planet Earth? You're not the only person in the world who has made a foolish mistake."

Roger bowed his head and said little more. Ricardo left, Roger went home, and the next day he started feeling better. A few weeks went by before his life would change.

Roger encountered Robin in the freezer section of a grocery store, near the ice cream. Robin, sweet Robin, in her early thirties, was a counselor at the local high school. She had auburn-colored hair that nested softly on her shoulders. Her eyes, more blue than green, had an ocean-like depth, and her curves were smooth, and her complexion…oh my!

"I can't decide between all these flavors of ice cream," said Roger, standing beside her, transparently attracted to this gem of a woman next to him.

She glanced at him more by swiveling her eyes than turning her head, barely suggesting a smile, yet with a warmth that could have melted the ice cream. He was ready for such a climate change.

"What's your favorite flavor?" he asked, hoping it wouldn't be vanilla, which he found too white.

"Double chocolate with hazelnuts," she said, without missing a beat.

"I'm Roger. And you…?"

"Robin."

"Robin," he repeated. "Hi."

He didn't tell her that he found her as delicate as a robin, harbinger of Spring and new beginnings. She was wearing a reddish-orange sweater, mimicking a robin's red breast. Roger bought a quart of double chocolate ice cream riddled with hazelnuts, suddenly his favorite flavor.

"Will you join me in dessert?" he asked, risking rejection.

There were many reasons for why she might refuse: maybe she was married (but she wasn't wearing a ring), maybe she was living with some guy (but then her smile might have been less inviting), maybe she was just reluctant to go out with strangers (but she was openly friendly).

"After that we can go to dinner," he said, with his fingers crossed. "I've always wanted to have dessert before the entrée."

That was true, but he'd never actually done it.

"Where shall we eat it?" she asked.

Yes!

"How about the bench across the street?" he said, straining to appear casual.

They polished off the quart of ice cream with two spoons racing to the finish line.

"Dinner now?" she asked.

After a stroll to digest dessert, they went to a small, cozy Italian restaurant for the entrée. That neither was the least bit hungry anymore made no difference. They shared a plate of spaghetti and meatballs and downed a bottle of red wine.

They dated for a month and developed an intimate relationship. Roger's life looked sunny again.

Ricardo stayed conspicuously absent.

After some time, however, dark clouds drifted in. There were lulls in their conversations, and private thoughts created gaps between them. They held hands infrequently when they walked side-by-side or sat together watching a movie. Robin was more carefree than he, and he blamed her for the growing distance. She became less available, they often disagreed in their opinions and preferences in movies and books, minor issues, true, but wasn't that what life was all about? Small stuff. Bread and butter. The busy hours of the days and the quiet moments of the nights. The gradual distancing in their relationship worried Roger. But he rationalized that relationships evolved even when people loved each other, and that no relationships were perfect.

Sensing an emergency, Ricardo made his appearance with matching orange socks. "This is serious, Roger. Robin isn't a research project that can be dropped or changed because of some data irregularities. What's your problem?"

Ricardo waited, almost defiantly, for an answer.

"She always wants me to do something with her and resents when I go to the laboratory. I can't do that, Ricardo. I can't let her destroy me in one way or another."

"Well, do you love her? What would your life be like without her?"

Silence. "Yes, and miserable," was Roger's answer.

"So, take her to the lab, then play."

Roger did just that. Surprisingly, the seas calmed. She loved the quiet time at the lab in the evenings and weekends, and Roger loved having her there. He set up a special corner with a coffee maker and comfortable chair for her, and he made it a point never to work longer than necessary. She read Tolstoy's *War and Peace*, and then *Anna Karenina*, and then Dostoevsky's *Brothers Karamazov* and *The Idiot*, while he worked. She also read Cervantes's *Don Quixote*, imagining, not without cause, the delusional knight errant – the valiant Don Quixote – would be a hero for Roger. When he finished his work at the lab, they usually went out to dinner, or a late snack, or even a late, late snack, often at that lovely little Italian restaurant where they had their first meal together. Sometimes they would go to a late movie afterwards. They loved movies, and they held hands again.

"How come you read all these Russian novels?" he asked her.

"Because they're interminably long and fill the time," she said, with her irresistible smile. "Your work doesn't end quickly! And these books are really good. I felt so sorry for Anna Karenina and…well, read the novels yourself. They're terrific. And you might read *Don Quixote* too, but don't take it personally!"

Although Ricardo stayed away as Roger and Robin became closer again, he did take note of their conversations. He was especially impressed by Robin's stressing Don Quixote, because he too thought that whacko, self-proclaimed knight was an accurate comparison with Roger. Also, Ricardo felt a bond with Cervantes, who is thought to have written part of the novel while in jail.

Roger read the novels, and he did think they were terrific, and Don Quixote did hit a raw nerve. He loved Robin more than ever, as she did him. They married and raised a bunch of children. How many doesn't matter for the present tale. Apart from some frivolous vacations and usual difficulties raising kids, the children had little to do with how his life unfolded.

Roger's mood soared as his family expanded, but his itch for adventure returned after a few years. He found his research too mainstream, not bold enough. He targeted small questions and published articles, but without risk, he felt dissatisfied. As before, he started flirting with the idea of working in the "wilderness of ignorance" – Ricardo's phrase – and chasing new concepts. But which ones?

The Golden Prize

When Roger's reputation as a scientist grew, he was invited to be on the panel that selected the winner of the coveted annual Golden Prize given by the prestigious Society for Research in Protein Structure and Function. As lucrative as the $50,000 award was, the honor of receiving the prize was worth considerably more than that. Recognitions and awards played a heavy hand in a scientist's career and scientific voice. Roger would be the youngest member of this panel, making it an honor to have been chosen to participate. The committee appointment was for three years. He proudly accepted.

In Roger's first meeting, the dozen panelists, all members of the society, eliminated all but two of the nominees for the award – Sam Leeman and Anthony Lunt. They represented polar opposites in their research and approach to science. Roger made it a point to remain open-minded and give equal consideration to each. He also had the good sense not to show too much enthusiasm for one or the other candidate. He didn't feel established or secure enough to be placed in any one scientific camp, which might make him ultimately lose support in the future – perhaps if he was considered for the Golden Prize. It was not only the candidates who were judged in such panels, but the panelists as well. Their opinions and views branded them in certain categories. Roger thought broadly and didn't want to be placed in any category. He wanted to appear neutral and open-minded.

Lunt's research focused on medical application, and his present contribution was on ALS – known as Lou Gehrig's Disease. Lunt's goal was to find a cure, or at least find better treatments for the devastating illness. Leeman, by contrast, was a basic scientist with no clear goal. He was on a scientific journey for knowledge, the so-called Ivory Tower of academia. His research was about transfer of chemicals between sponge cells. Leeman's encompassing view concerned the foundations and evolution of biological processes. His work was about health, not illness, although, as in all basic research, the cellular transfer system he had discovered would, hopefully, become relevant for some application.

Roger favored Leeman, a staunch basic scientist, who sought questions rather than answers. Like Roger, Leeman preferred to blaze new trails than to travel those already crowded.

Despite the background noise of the committee's discussions, Ricardo privately taunted Roger.

"Hey, don't let these guys eliminate Leeman because he hasn't decided prematurely on a specific destination to his research journey. It seems to me that he doesn't know enough yet to target potential endpoints." Then Ricardo, as not uncommon for him, started to ramble poetically. "Face it, if you don't notice the scenery, how do you know where you are?"

"Quiet, please!" Roger silently begged Ricardo. "I can't listen to the committee's discussions if you keep chatting."

Ricardo kept yakking in Roger's mind, distracting him. Damn him sometimes!

"What do you think?" the committee chairman asked Carl Freeman, one of the panelists. "Do you think that Sam's research opens new research approaches worthy of the award? His work is certainly unique."

Carl, a respected scientist, was generally willing to consider new ideas. Apart from being impeccably polite, Carl was also the only person on the committee who always wore a tie. In Roger's opinion that may have been old-fashioned, but it set him apart, perhaps ironically more independent than the others, as superficial and counterintuitive as that was. Carl had won the Golden Prize five years earlier for a mouse protein that appeared to be a marker for glaucoma. A few years later, however, Carl's protein popped up in several other tissues, casting doubt on its significance as a glaucoma marker. Rather than act defensively, Carl wrote an article stressing how important it was to investigate thoroughly the basic science of what's observed rather than bending prematurely to a subjective preference.

Roger hoped Carl would support Leeman. He was the type that might.

"Sam's a pioneer. Fine fellow," Carl said, in his soft-spoken, velvet-like voice, almost angelic, which made him appear objective. But then he hesitated and scanned the faces of his peers.

William Sloan, the outspoken and influential winner of last year's prize, shook his head very slightly.

Klara Richardson, a junior member of the panel in her early thirties, kept sneaking glances at her mobile phone on her lap.

Carl continued. "That bizarre protein that Sam discovered in sponges – what's it called? Slingshot? I can't remember... interesting name, anyway, it may be important someday...yes, I think so...maybe. Sponges are animals, aren't they?"

Roger was disappointed by Carl's wishy-washy comments. Sponges are animals? Did he think that sponges were objects? Anything but praise was damning for the candidate. Even a slightly negative comment outweighed a host of positives: "No" always outdid "Yes." It was like art: one doubt about authenticity by a critic was far more damaging than the support of authenticity by several other critics was positive.

"You don't sound very enthusiastic, Carl?" said Sol Spiegle, clearly frustrated. Sol was a trustworthy supporter of Leeman. Roger hoped that he would be more supportive for him, although he worried that Sol might go off on a tangent. He was bright but tended to ramble off track, which diluted his support.

Ricardo picked that up immediately and told Roger, "It's like a defense trial. I should know! The more said, the more chance you put your foot in your mouth. Defense lawyers always tell their client to say as little as they can get away with, and nothing if possible."

Sol continued. "Probably Sam calls it 'Slingshot' because its structure is Y-shaped and it implies that it 'slings' molecules from cell to cell, at least that's what Sam told me. That name is as good as anything else. I'd place it in a new category of proteins and possibly a new pathway for transferring molecules between cells. Good stuff. Important."

Sol supported Leeman, but everyone knew that he was Sam Leeman's friend, and friends support each other. Nothing could be done about such favoritism; it was an occupational reality. Scientists were cronies who knew each other for years. Remaining objective in such an environment was nearly impossible.

"Maybe, Sol," said Carl, in his deceptively quiet tone. "Yet, few people cite his studies – and sponges? We're not marine biologists and don't want to look foolish. Can you name a single sponge disease?"

Snickers sprinkled around the oval table, as if summoning Ricardo, who appeared and took the bait.

"Here we go again, ridiculing imaginative work just because it lacks absolute proof yet. I've been there once, and that's enough for me," he muttered, standing next to the water cooler.

Roger was livid. Sponge diseases? What next? That was unlike smooth Carl. We're not veterinarians! Then, to keep Sam's chances alive, Roger told the panel, in a neutral voice, "That few people cite Sam's work doesn't mean it isn't important and significant. Sam's not a network type of guy. Let's not penalize him because of that."

His comment was met with silence. Carl's eyes remained downcast, and Klara stopped fiddling with her phone and started doodling on scrap paper.

With Carl's reference to marine biology, Roger thought of the time he had snorkeled in the coral reef in Australia. How extraordinary that was! The beauty, the mystery beneath the surface! Sadly, now it was dying due to climate change and pollution by thoughtless people who didn't care, or even realize the harm they were doing. That's what happens when no one considers seriously unseen phenomena below the surface, too ignorant to realize that if life in the ocean – three-quarters of the planet – dies, then we're done for too. It was infuriating. *Indifference* was the worst sin of all because it's invisible.

Ignorance and narrow views. Sponges didn't seem serious science to the panelists. Looking around at the committee members, Roger read their faces: they said, goodbye, Sam.

"Well," the chairman said, after what felt like a lengthy pause, "What about Anthony Lunt, our other candidate? Tony's always in the limelight."

Roger noted Carl doing his best to cover his smile.

"He's on the leading edge, for sure," volunteered Mark, with a jolt of energy belying his dull eyes. Mark and Tony were close friends. "You all know his discovery of the protein he calls LG because it was discovered in cells from a patient with Lou Gehrig's disease. Tony is convinced it's an important marker for that dreaded illness. He received the coveted Arlington Award last year for that work, if you remember. He's a long-term loyal member of our organization and overdue for this award. Tony's a good man. I give him a 10; he's my guy."

Nods went around the table.

Mark settled back in his chair, avoiding eye contact with anyone else.

Yes, we know, thought Roger. Protein LG again. He agreed that Lou Gehrig's disease was a horrible illness. Anything else new? Always good to hear what you already knew, or thought you knew.

Ricardo appeared in the corner of the room and said matter-of-factly, "Protein LG might not even have a role in the illness and, in my humble opinion, is no more revealing than announcing that exercise is good for you."

Roger, feeling discouraged, nodded to Ricardo in agreement. Protein LG again. Anything else new?

Linda, the astute department head of medicine at Washington University Medical School, broke Roger's thoughts by telling the panel of a patient who died of Lou Gehrig's disease last year. "I wish I could have helped him," she said. "Maybe Tony's protein has an important role that could be targeted with a drug someday."

"Or maybe not," said Ricardo, and then he disappeared.

Roger's mind flashed back to marine organisms. How did sponges sense their environment? Were jellyfish immune to cancer, like sharks? Did any invertebrate get dementia, and if so, how was it manifested? There were so many mysteries in nature. Why did so many scientists investigate similar problems? What about that intriguing "wilderness of ignorance"?

"That's right, Roger," mused Ricardo in Roger's mind.

"Time to vote, ladies and gentlemen," said the chairman, late in the afternoon. "Rate each candidate between 1 and 10, with 10 the best, as always. The person with the highest score is our Golden Prize awardee for next year. Vote your conscience, then pass your choice up front."

The vote was tallied. Roger knew it was a foregone conclusion. Anthony Lunt's ball was rolling – 8 to 2 in his favor. Roger sighed. So much for innovation.

"Mark, could you please call your friend Tony and congratulate him. I'll send a formal acknowledgment to him," the chairman said.

Mark nodded and suppressed a victory glow that Roger did his best to ignore.

The panelists chit-chatted about weekend plans, recent movies, the National's disastrous baseball losing streak and the like as they gathered their belongings. Science vaporized. Tony Lunt? No more interest. Sam Leeman? Maybe next year. They had a winner. Lunt again. Good job, no? Famous scientist confirmed. So much for that. History.

Roger wondered if Sol would tell his friend that he was in the Final 2. No, maybe he wouldn't. No one likes to be number 2.

Dinner with Nathan

At dinner that night, Roger sat with ~~Roger sat with~~ his colleague Nathan in a booth in their favorite rural restaurant where they often ate together. Roger, clearly dispirited, related the gossip at the award committee – what was said, who spoke up for whom, the usual shop talk.

"So, Tony wins again," Nathan said, before ordering a scoop of chocolate ice cream for dessert.

"That's about it," said Roger. "Funny thing is that I think most of the committee members, if asked separately, would say that Sam's work was more original, more daring and more likely to have impact over time. And after all his years of contributions, he deserves recognition. Wouldn't you prefer to have had the foresight to predict new directions than simply flow with the current? But Mark drove the vote to his friend Anthony Lunt. Tony was a safe choice, but certainly not a bold one. No one likes to stick their neck out. Peer pressure, I guess. Too bad."

"You okay, Roger?"

"Sure. Why do you ask?"

"You sound bitter. You're sort of…I don't know…looking defeated. There's nothing wrong with Tony. Protein LG *is* interesting, and he's a deserving scientist."

"I know, but everyone seems reluctant to do something different, more daring. How many times do I have to say it? Discovery means finding something new, which requires a certain amount of risk and courage. There's a difference between forging a new path and taking a step forward on a cleared one. It's Robert Frost's *The Road Less Taken* that really does make a difference."

"Come on. We've been through this before. Awards reflect the current state of science. It doesn't predict it. Life goes on. Slingshot, I admit that's a crazy name for a protein, and it may be important someday. Who knows? Sam's got more work to do, that's all."

"Yeah, I guess," said Roger, who seemed disconnected. He was looking at a mother wiping her infant's face with a napkin at the next table.

"Roger? Hello."

Still quiet, Roger gazed out the plate glass window and watched the purplish-red sun splashing colors as it plunged below the tree landscape. Sunset.

"The dying day is preparing for tomorrow's dawn," he muttered.

Suddenly, as if a magic key had opened an invisible lock, Roger straightened in his seat and squinted, as he often did when bemused with a new idea. Nathan wrinkled his brow seeming confused about his friend's wavering mood.

"Nathan, we've done pretty well, wouldn't you say? After all, we're still relative newcomers as scientists, yet have tenure and are known by our peers. But we've hardly set the world aflame. And I don't think Tony Lunt has either, but you sure wouldn't know that from all the hoopla he's receiving."

"What are you getting at?" asked Nathan. "Envious?"

"We follow like sheep, Nathan," Roger said, "at least I seem to. Why didn't I speak up more forcefully in favor of Sam

Leeman? Maybe I could have changed some minds by saying what I truly think, not hiding behind what others expect, afraid to look foolish or not in sync with the times. Do you really think that 1% of the people deserve 99% of the honors? That's what happens, you know. It's recognition inequality! It's the same guys over and over again, and then their students and... well, is that what you mean when you keep saying, life goes on?"

"Why are you so bitter, Roger? You're among the winners, at least the promising winners."

"I don't feel that way," Roger said. "I feel on the fringe, like a seashell on wet sand at low tide. Kind of stuck, immobile, a puppet of the tide."

"I don't follow."

The restaurant suddenly started swirling around in Roger's head and funny clicking sounds hammered in his brain.

"Roger, are you okay? You look pale."

"Hold off a minute, Nathan. I'm dizzy and nauseous. Is it something I ate? No, we had the same dish. Are you okay?"

"Yeah," Nathan nodded.

Roger slumped in his chair for a moment and put his head down to let the blood rush to his brain.

"It's better. I'm less lightheaded. Things are returning to normal. What do you think that was? A mini-stroke?" Roger looked scared, took a deep breath and closed his eyes for a moment.

"I don't know, hopefully nothing serious," said Nathan. "Probably just stress. But if it happens again, I'd have a doctor check it out. So...what were you saying?"

Roger took a deep breath and continued. Nathan was right. He had often had such brief dizzy spells when he felt stressed.

"What if I stopped twisting myself into a contortionist trying to be fair – to be objective – to keep my mind open to every alternative – in short, to be politically correct all the time, like I did at the award committee. I didn't fight for my convictions. When sponges were ridiculed, I was no better than one myself in response. When Mark pushed his buddy Tony, I should have challenged him to explain why he thought more of the same from Tony was preferable to something new by Sam. I avoided contradicting anyone and was careful to blend with what others might think about me. How lame is that! If I had pushed back a bit, at least I would have felt honest or more significant."

"Really?" said Nathan, not seeming convinced that whatever Roger had said would have made much difference.

Roger felt the blood return to his face. He wished he didn't care so much about the opinions of others. If only he could be an independent spirit, his own man, but...he *did* care. He wondered if anyone truly didn't care what others thought about them? Wouldn't *that* be self-centered, extremely so, thinking that the opinions of other people didn't matter? Wouldn't indifference to that be the highest form of self-centeredness? Yes, it would. Indifference was a powerful force. Was Jean-Paul Sartre's rejection of the Nobel Prize a sign of humility or the need to remain independent, when he said that he didn't want to be institutionalized, that his writing and creativity would suffer if he was associated with any group. Or did it mean that he was above it all, suspended above everyone, above the Nobel Prize? Wouldn't that be even greater self-praise than simply saying, "Thank you," and moving on?

Nathan frowned. "Should we order another bottle of wine, or something stronger?"

He was used to Roger going astray – globalizing, Robin called it – in his thoughts, which were often interesting and imaginative, even if unconventional. They were friends since college, professional colleagues, and close companions. Roger was Roger, just as Nathan was Nathan, and so be it.

Roger continued, searching for an idea.

"A tree is pretty much ignored as it grows slowly over many years, but it can be chopped down in minutes," he said. "Impressive how much noise and attention it receives crashing to the ground, if anyone is watching, that is, and somebody always seems to be."

"Go on. I'm lost," said Nathan, scratching his head, accustomed to Roger's free associating.

"That's it, Nathan. I'll use a metaphorical axe, chop the trees down and not worry about how much noise they make – how much attention they receive – when crashing to the ground."

Nathan looked directly into Roger's eyes, curious to understand what he was trying to say. Strange, yet…he felt a meaningful undertow.

"It's suicidal…I don't know… nobody does…that's the point. Everything is subjective, just like who gets an award and who doesn't: who flatters and gets rewarded, who criticizes and gets ignored, and the reverse, who insults and gets elected. Everyone knows politicians who have made careers by slandering and lying, and then winning! Go figure."

"Suicidal" stuck in Roger's mind. What exactly was professional suicide – making oneself unpopular? Insulting the powers that be? Death in one scene may be birth in another, he thought, without understanding exactly what he was saying.

"You've got to make more sense than that, Roger. I still don't get it."

"I'm figuring it out myself, Nathan, figuring out what I mean. Awards are partly recognition for the work, but they're also political, and all that politics imply. I recall reading years ago that John Steinbeck wrote a letter after receiving the Nobel

Prize for literature and said that professional recognitions were as much to honor the source of the award – the person or organization – whoever or whatever that was – as to honor the awardee. Giving the award could be even more prestigious than receiving it. I think he's right in a way. Look at philanthropists. Heroes! Icons! Everyone knows the Nobel Prize, the generosity and values of Mr. Nobel. How many people know the various people who won it? Perhaps that's debatable, but I get it. It's the same for anyone in a creative endeavor. Lucky awardee, but the top echelon is the awarder, the donor, the source that makes it possible. But what about those who go out on a limb, catalyze ideas and inspire others to be bold and take chances – the guys with a machete who blaze the path and provide the foundations for progress by others? When are they recognized and by whom? They're like the dark matter of creativity and progress."

"You're going in circles and asking a lot of questions, Roger. What's bothering you so much?"

"Why is Tony Lunt on a pedestal and Sam Leeman in the cellar?"

"That's all?"

"No, there's more. I'm curious about how ideas develop and how trends are established, not just who committees deem best…and…"

Roger stopped in midstream trying to crystallize the muddle in his head. Nathan gave him space to do so.

After a short pause, Roger said, "What makes people think the way they do? What is it, Nathan? Peer pressure? Lack of imagination, or abundance of it? Previous experiences? Genes? What's a thought and why are they contagious?"

"Contagious? Wow, strange question, Roger. You should have been a psychiatrist. Are you serious, or still dizzy? Maybe you need a vacation to go fishing or something."

Roger considered Nathan's skepticism. "Hmm, a psychiatrist. Really? Do they have the answers? I'm serious, at least at the moment. I guess this is fishing in a way. I'm fishing for something, even though I don't know what the fish is yet. I'm thinking of removing the filters and saying what I feel at the moment."

"What do you mean?"

It's at times like this that Roger wanted Ricardo to appear and join the conversation. But no such luck. He was out of touch, neither dependable nor predictable. Sometimes he came, sometimes he didn't. The guy was his own boss.

Roger looked confused.

"What's wrong, Roger?"

"I don't know," muttered Roger. "Maybe this is more complicated than I thought. Opinions can be fluid and flow any which way, from hero to villain, from teacher to student and back again, as the breeze changes direction. I wonder…people are reluctant to go against the tide and can believe almost anything. It's hard to understand. Isn't public opinion just a large committee on parade? It seems infectious."

"People can believe almost anything? Infectious opinions? What did you say?" Nathan asked, leaning forward trying to understand.

"Say? Nothing. Forget it," Roger said.

"Roger, you're the only person I know who can prick your toe on a needle in a haystack."

Roger smiled. Yes, maybe that was it: he always found the needle in a haystack that injured him.

And then Nathan concentrated on his ice cream while Roger sipped his coffee.

Roger's Outburst

After his dinner with Nathan, Roger drifted in and out of the laboratory the next month with little enthusiasm. He attended laboratory meetings and fulfilled bureaucratic duties, all routine. When Robin asked him how the day had gone when he returned home from the laboratory, Roger answered, "Fine," as all school kids do when asked how school was that day. Each day was a continuation of the day before, nothing special. It was "fine." Or perhaps it required too much effort to explain exactly what had happened. "Fine" was the most economical answer that deflected the question.

It was the same with Robin. When Roger asked about her day counseling high school kids, she would say, "As usual," although she generally threw in something of interest that occupied her mind. It may have been as mundane as an adolescent girl upset about being teased by the other girls that her shoes didn't match the rest of her attire; or, it could have been more serious, such as a boy struggling academically; and on occasion it might have been alarming, like a desperate child crying out for help from an abusive parent. Each case involved a situation that had not existed in exactly the same way before in her life.

Life marches on uneventfully day after day for most people. That's the way it is, yet no day is quite the same as any before.

Different experiences, whether of little note or more consequential, ultimately blend with one another to create a distinct life for each individual.

One day, Dr. Thomas, the Scientific Director of the Vision Science Center, called Roger and asked him to come to his office to discuss an important matter. Although irritated to feel he was at the beck and call of his boss, Roger complied and went to Dr. Thomas's office.

"Careful," Ricardo warned as Roger was on his way. "I've been there, same institution, same problems. A few generations apart don't change the ballgame."

"Don't worry," said Roger.

"What's up?" Roger said as he entered his boss's office, trying to sound upbeat. Dr. Thomas sat on the padded chair behind his cluttered desk, and Roger took the hard-back chair facing the desk.

"Your laboratory is being reviewed next week by the outside committee and, as you know, these reviews are sent to Congress and affect future funding. I thought it would be helpful if we could go over what you are going to tell them. I need to be sure you will represent us well."

Roger didn't blink, but he felt the pressure, like steam gathering in a boiling teapot before tripping the valve to escape. He had never been questioned about his research in a manner suggesting that he might have poor judgment or what he might tell the reviewers.

Ricardo flashed before him looking angry and prophetic at the same time. "See what I mean?"

Roger was a seasoned scientist and knew how to play the game. He took Dr. Thomas's comments as micromanagement, which, no doubt, was what Ricardo warned him about a moment ago, how he too had been quizzed by his Scientific Director in a similar manner over 100 years ago. Although Ricardo had considered this unacceptable micromanagement, he had reacted diplomatically.

Dr. Thomas didn't notice Roger blanching to ghost-white, and his transformation didn't stop there. He felt shaky, hollow and lightheaded. Something was going on he couldn't control. Furious, he heard threatening sirens in his mind – an unsettling cacophony – and he exploded.

The opportunity to ask a person flattened by a locomotive whether he had heard the oncoming train and, if so, what he was thinking, is gone. That transient instant is lost forever, like the thoughts of a person whose brain is splattered like spaghetti upon impact after falling off a cliff on rocks. Questions remain unanswered forever. For example, did he jump on purpose, or did he slip? If he had jumped, why? Did he regret it? Or was it an accident? Or perhaps he was pushed. If it was murder, who committed the crime? Was he thinking about anything as he was falling to his demise? Yes, what was he thinking as he was hurling to the ground?

Roger suddenly screamed internally with anger that soared with wings of freedom, away from the drab mist outside, past the dying leaves of Fall, up and up, above the clouds, into the dark nothingness of space, away from the claws of gravity, in which weight reflects the attraction of the planet's mass, not just that of the subject. Roger suddenly felt alive, 30 again, maybe younger. He floated. He spoke his heart in no uncertain words:

"Dr. Thomas, what do you know of my work, about what it really means or implies? How could you? You just sit at your desk in that whiter than white lab coat that never passed a minute through a laboratory. Its only stain is ink leaked from the pens clipped in the breast pocket. What gall you have to look me in the eye and

cast judgment! What nerve to even think you know what I should tell the royal committee, who dare to promote themselves at my expense! I'm not going to tell you what I plan to tell them, because I don't even know yet. And if I did, I still wouldn't tell you. I don't care what you think I should tell them. Your fate depends on my decisions, not your desires. Put that in your teacup. Ha! Goodbye for now, and my best to your lovely wife."

Shocking!

Standing next to him in awe, Ricardo said, "I wish I'd said that to my prosecutor!"

Roger had expressed his truth at that moment, the way he saw the oppressive world. Rude? Certainly! Appropriate? No! But no more resenting in silence. He had opened the dam holding back the tsunami. Had he committed professional suicide, the beginning of the end for his career? Perhaps. If that was his destiny, so be it. He didn't have a life jacket. It was sink or swim. And then, as if in a dream with all the qualities of a nightmare, Roger pranced out of Dr. Thomas's office, paraded past Shirley, the executive assistant, who looked up confused. He went into the hallway at a steady pace, as if he were a battery-operated toy soldier, on his way back to his office, staring straight ahead, his upper lip quivering, his left hand, the dominant one, trembling, his heart palpitating – boom, boom, boom – feeling feather-light, yet weighted down as if by a boulder pressing on his shoulders, with tears of joy mixed with fear cleansing his soul like never before.

Roger had turned the corner of his life. There was no returning, or so he believed. He was doing his best to control himself, but the storm inside wouldn't subside.

Dr. Thomas, drained whiter than his lab coat, sat speechless at his desk in his office, upset, furious, probably as furious as Roger had been, maybe even more so, but for different reasons, and not able to let it escape, as Roger had. Although no one but Dr. Thomas himself could possibly know exactly what it was like to be him, it's likely that his bewilderment wasn't all anger. He must have also felt vulnerable, as judged from what happened later. Vulnerable, that must have been it. Was this for real? Roger, his poster scientist, the prize of the department. What in the world...? Why?

Shirley knocked on his door. "Dr. Thomas...are you okay? Is everything all right? Dr. Resin just stormed out. May I come in?"

"I'm fine...no problem, Shirley...a slight misunderstanding. I'm busy, need to meet a deadline before lunch."

"Are you sure? Can I get you something?" Shirley had worked for Dr. Thomas for a dozen years and was fond of him. She had never before seen him like this.

"Sure, yes, I'm fine. No, I don't need anything. Thank you."

He wasn't going to let her in. He needed to be by himself, he *had* to be by himself to re-equilibrate and figure out what just happened.

"Okay, sir."

Such fear and self-doubt mixed with despair wasn't new to Dr. Thomas. He felt like an adolescent being criticized by his father for never taking a stand on what he believed, always being diplomatic, joining the consensus of others. He heard his father's voice saying, "If you're everyone's friend, you're no one's friend."

Had he been Roger's friend? What had he said or done wrong? It was his job to make sure the research in the department attracted funds. Roger knew that. Why did he explode? He assumed Roger knew how valuable he was for the department...strange. All Dr. Thomas wanted was to know what

Roger had planned to tell the reviewing committee. What was wrong with that? What should he do now? Reach out to Roger and try to mollify him, win him back? If so, should he reach out now or wait to let them both cool down? Maybe he should ignore the outburst altogether? No, that would be weak. Maybe he should strike back? Is it true that a strong offense is the best defense? But this wasn't a football game. How to keep the peace? How to be a boss and a friend too? Was it possible? Was it even desirable?

Glowing Review

Roger checked his emails when he returned to his office, relieved that Dr. Thomas hadn't already struck back somehow. He feared that his budget might be slashed, or that laboratory space would be taken from him for a new departmental initiative, a common means of downgrading, if not actually forcing out tenured staff. Losing everything he had worked for his entire professional life was easier to fantasize about than endure. Was he committing professional suicide, for what, why?

But nothing happened. Not a thing. Ricardo didn't even appear.

The director didn't get in touch with him. He assumed no one except Shirley knew about the freak outburst. It had happened behind closed doors, after all, and Roger had kept it to himself. But did Dr. Thomas? Probably. Maybe. Maybe not. It wouldn't be to Thomas's advantage to advertise the ugly scene, would it?

The laboratory review came and went. One of the panelists suggested that Roger terminate his research on a novel earthworm protein he had discovered by chance, a side project that he worked on slowly now and then, independently, not with his postdoctoral fellows. It wasn't a major project, but a personal detour that Roger found fascinating. After all, research is exploration to see what's out there, no? Testing the waters, so to speak.

"It's too undefined," the reviewer had said. "Where is this worm protein research heading? What's the point? You can't just spend money on everything that *might* be interesting."

"What's the point?" Roger had repeated to himself, reacting with annoyance to the criticism. "What's the point of gaining knowledge about a novel protein? Why not ask what's the point of basic research?"

"Well, Roger, this is déjà vu for me," said Ricardo, when he suddenly appeared glaring defiantly into space. "I was jailed for doing what was called irrelevant research. Imagine, basic science considered *irrelevant*! That's what knowledge was for critics who just didn't 'get it' in my day. At least they don't do that anymore. But still…the more things change, the more they stay the same."

Roger had felt on the verge of exploding again, possibly this time with more reason than he had for his string of insults to Dr. Thomas, but he caught himself in time. Good for him. Risking his career with a damaging review that paints him an opinionated scientist with a closed mind was not worth the immediate gratification of being a pariah who says it as he sees it. Not now, not right after he lost his composure with the scientific director. He thought it best to gloss over the criticism. There were too many other people in his laboratory who could be hurt by confronting a member of the review panel. Self-destruction was one thing; harming innocent associates was another. Roger may have had self-destructive instincts, but he never wanted to damage or endanger anyone else.

"Perhaps you're right. I'll consider dropping the project," Roger had said to the critical reviewer, with no intention what- soever of doing so, and then he proceeded to give an objective, dispassionate account of his recent work, nothing off-beat, keeping the worms underground where the reviewers thought they belonged. Business as usual. Conventional. Safe.

Life went on, just as Nathan always said. Just like that. The river keeps flowing, yet the water looks the same, although it's always different, fresh.

A few weeks later Roger received the panel's review. He'd hoped for a supportive review – at least a rubber stamp to show that his research was a benefit to the institution – coupled with a few minor suggestions. But that didn't happen. There was no bland rubber stamp saying "interesting, good job, keep it up, but change so and so." The review did not reflect the passing grade with "room for improvement" he had expected.

Nothing like that. The report glowed, literally sparkled! Spectacular! Excellent! It was more favorable and superlative than he believed was appropriate. He was thrilled, who wouldn't be? Who doesn't like praise? But this was plain flattery, inconsistent with what Roger thought he deserved, and he started to question why. Where was the needle in this haystack? The reviewers suggested that his work was on the edge of a "breakthrough." Breakthrough to what? He knew that his research was sound at this stage, but really…it wasn't "spellbinding," as the panelists wrote, at least not yet, and it might never be. He had made consistently small contributions throughout his career, and that was still the case in his opinion. Why wasn't there any mention of the earthworm protein, which had been challenged? Did they no longer care whether or not he continued that project?

The other members of his laboratory were ecstatic. "That's terrific, Roger. Wow. Congratulations," they said. "We're in great shape."

"Thanks, yes, but honestly, do you think we've really done so much?"

"Yeah, we're moving. Aren't you happy about this?" said his technician, beaming. "Who knows how important new knowledge is? Isn't that your mantra, Roger? Everyone has a different opinion, and the reviewers' written opinion is critically important for us to be funded," she said.

A writer friend with whom Roger often socialized during weekends had a similar reaction. "Enjoy it. No matter what, you always think you haven't done enough, whether ignored or praised," he said. "It's hard to please you!"

"I was lucky," was Roger's response.

But it was Robin's opinion Roger most wanted, and she was thrilled. "That's wonderful, Roger," she said. "Let's celebrate!"

They did, with a quiet dinner at that Italian restaurant.

Nathan's comment, that Roger could prick his toe on a needle in a haystack, flashed through his mind again. It was true: if there was a flaw to be found, no matter how small or how buried – a metaphorical needle – he would find it. Damn that sharp needle. Stress was Roger's habitual state. Most of the time nothing was quite right for him. He often considered praise undeserved.

"Pity," Ricardo had said sarcastically, implying that Roger said he preferred to be criticized than praised, "I prefer an abundance of praise myself, any amount that keeps me out of jail."

Roger wondered whether his insults to Dr. Thomas had leaked to the panel, resulting in their reluctance to irritate him. Ridiculous. Why would they care or want to placate him if they did know about it? Yet, the possibility – speculative at best – that the reviewers did know about Roger's outburst with Dr. Thomas and thought it was important to keep harmony within the department had a certain allure: being "bad" to get "good". Roger never expected that his anger would enhance his standing with Dr. Thomas. He expected the reverse. Neither had he strategically planned his outburst in order to advance himself. Receiving praise for insults? Really?

Roger tossed and turned most of the night thinking about his report, not because of anger or disappointment, of course, but because of success. What was going through Dr. Thomas's mind when he read this report?

He found out the next day when he received an email from Dr. Thomas congratulating him for the superlative review. "We're proud of you," he said, with no mention of Roger's meltdown.

Amazing! But strange too.

A few days later Roger heard from his colleague Henry, who occupied the laboratory next to his, that Dr. Thomas was concerned whether Roger was well or had some personal problems.

"Why was that?" Henry asked. "What's Thomas referring to?"

Roger told him about his outburst. "I lost it, Henry. I don't know, I'm tired of walking on eggs, to be a pebble on the beach that people trample on, to be predictable, to be a 'yes man.'"

Henry told Roger that Dr. Thomas had looked worried and that he, Roger, was very important for the department, that he wanted to establish a special university-wide award for scholarship and thought that Roger should be the first awardee.

"You're a lucky guy, Roger. Everything goes your way," said Henry, sounding envious.

Since Henry never mentioned anything about confidentiality, and Dr. Thomas knew that he and Roger had adjacent laboratories and saw each other frequently, Roger thought that maybe Dr. Thomas wanted him to hear about the prospective award.

"Is that true?" Roger asked, perplexed. "Getting an award for insulting the boss?"

"I doubt it was for your outburst; more likely it's in spite of it."

"Really? Maybe."

Roger didn't hear anything more from Dr. Thomas about the ugly scene or any rumor about the award. Maybe the award wasn't serious or maybe it didn't pan out for some reason or other. Politics in science was an enigma within a puzzle, as was academia in all fields. Oh well, it didn't matter. Life goes on, as Nathan says. It always does.

Then, in the Spring, Roger became the first recipient of the new University Award for Outstanding Scholarship.

"Congratulations to our star and first Outstanding Scholar Awardee," Dr. Thomas said, toasting Roger at a reception in his office, smiling from ear to ear.

Henry winked at Roger and mouthed silently, "See?"

What's Real?

Despite Roger's unexpected award, his mood was spiraling downward. Perhaps he was overtired. Yet, a tinge of excitement percolated through his vulnerable soul, as if he was on an adventure of an indeterminate nature, although he knew that adventures could be dangerous. Ricardo had proved the unexpected danger of adventures with his jellyfish research.

Roger was restless for hours at night, unable to sleep. When he finally dozed off, he recurringly dreamed that he was alone lecturing in an auditorium filled with empty chairs. His voice sounded like a monotonous echo chamber that bounced off the walls. He was projecting images, as he always did in his lectures, but most of them were blank, which panicked him. He must have had something new to show, but what? Why were the slides blank? Perhaps because there was no audience. That both saddened and infuriated him: Roger needed an audience.

But not every slide was blank. One repeated in italics what he had hurled at Dr. Thomas: ...*I don't care what you think I should tell them. Your fate depends on my decisions...not your desires.*

In reality, Roger did care what Dr. Thomas thought, and Dr. Thomas's fate didn't depend on his decisions. As these contradictory feelings coursed through Roger's dreaming brain, Dr.

Thomas, smiling, handed him the diploma of his University Award for Outstanding Scholarship.

Roger always awoke anxious and angry, but his anger was tempered with a sense of freedom, as he had felt during his outburst in Dr. Thomas's office. Intertwining anger, anxiety, sadness and freedom were inseparable in the fog of Roger's outlook. He didn't know which emotion, if any, dominanted. Maybe it didn't matter. His was a life in progress.

But wait. Could this dream have an encrypted message? Maybe showing slides with no images in an auditorium with no audience meant that he had never insulted Dr. Thomas; maybe it was all his imagination – a hallucination. If so, no wonder Dr. Thomas wasn't mad at him and had even given him an award.

Ricardo materialized from thin air and said, "Forget about it, Roger. You gave Dr. Thomas the hell he deserved. I wish I had done the same with my scientific director. Maybe I would have been given an award instead of a prison sentence."

What was reality, Roger wondered. What was imagination and what was hallucination?

The Study Section

Roger spent the next month reviewing research proposals for a study section, where a panel of scientists selected which of the submitted proposals would receive grants. Appointment to a study section was for four years and considered an honor given to experts in their field of science, or perhaps more realistically, an underhanded honor, since it demanded that the panelists squeeze a great deal of work and responsibility into their already crowded schedules, pro bono. Roger was in his third year on the study section on basic biomedical science.

Whenever the heavy bundle of grants to be reviewed arrived in the mail, Roger's heart sank a notch, and he wondered why he had agreed to be on the panel. It eroded valuable time from his research and forced him to study side topics that he would have gladly ignored. Nevertheless, he accepted; it kept him abreast of the latest scientific developments, widened his scope of knowledge, and allowed him to serve as a good Samaritan, to help the society of scientists in which he lived. Still another reason for joining the study section panel tied in directly with his frustration with committees deciding who gets recognized with awards. He wanted to support the higher risk and more imaginative proposals that were seldom favored by the other panelists.

As with all conflicted decisions, Roger had personal, ambitious reasons that simmered beneath the surface for accepting the invitation to join the study section. He believed that being on a study section would raise his professional profile, enhance his all-important professional network, and increase his chances of gaining entrance, which meant being accepted by the inner circle of elites - the prestigious national academies and organizations comprising lucky individuals in the flux of scientists with the greatest visibility.

"Look at me," Ricardo muttered in Roger's ear. "I was praised and given awards for my research yet jailed as an irresponsible scientist for my groundbreaking research on jellyfish. Only my one true friend, Benjamin, a future Nobel laureate no less, came to my rescue, and he failed to be helpful. What kind of elite inner circle is that? Beware of shadows, Roger. Not all images have substance."

Roger lived in parallel universes. In one, he did belong to the cream at the top, the privileged and enlightened, who were sufficiently respected to appear modest and humble. As a tenured scientist at the prestigious Vision Science Center, as Ricardo had been in his era, Roger was invited to give keynote lectures at symposia, he had young postdoctoral scientists apply to him to be their mentor, and he received his share of honors. Although he understood the culture of doing to others as you would have them do unto you – to scratch their back so they would scratch yours when the need arose – he had never abused the principle. He never felt he needed to. Also, he never felt confident that his support was particularly effective.

In the other universe, Roger was an underdog, a hidden, unrecognized soul, a longshot to win a significant award, at least not in his lifetime. He hoped that there would be room for recognition later, after death, when his legacy might brighten, and it would become clear his work had been unfairly ignored. Considering himself part of this lower echelon of scientists – the second tier, at best – Roger was nervous when the study section met, afraid that he would appear naïve or foolish in defending a grant request filled with flaws or in rejecting one that was considered outstanding by the other members of the panel.

Poor Roger. On one hand, he felt entitled to cast judgment, yet on the other hand he was scared to do so, always feeling the need to prove himself.

Roger sat at the large oval table with the other members of the reviewing committee, all respected scientists, waiting for the arduous process to begin. He was checking his notes and arranging the proposals to be evaluated into thematic stacks. The apparent informality and socializing of the panelists about to deliberate which proposals merited funding didn't fool anyone. It was serious business: which projects were accepted, which were rejected, and most problematical, which ones were in between those categories – interesting, but not completely convincing – on the fence – one side acceptable and the other side… questionable. Being funded was critical for advancing the careers of the scientists (and for their survival as researchers) as well as for the direction of science. The deliberations at the meeting were strictly confidential; it was understood that the panelists would not reveal the discussions and decisions to their colleagues.

The chairperson, Dr. James Whipple, a self-assured, opinionated man in his sixties, called the meeting to order. Each grant request had a primary reviewer who gave a detailed criticism of the proposal, which was followed by a secondary reviewer who was more concise and either supported or challenged the primary reviewer's evaluation. The group then discussed the proposal.

Roger was the primary reviewer on a request to support a project on yeast biochemistry, which required more background knowledge of yeast than he had. He didn't feel comfortable casting judgment on it. What if he praised the proposal that others found poor, or vice-versa? As in committees judging who gets awards, harsh comments carried more weight than positive comments could overrule. Bad triumphed over good, except in rare cases.

Roger was never certain who was really being judged in these sessions, the proposer or the reviewer. Certainly both, in their own way, as in the award committees. Science was one thing, but the profession of science was something else entirely, which tended to wear him down.

The morning proceeded without incident. The yeast proposal came and went, with the other reviewer agreeing with Roger's positive opinion. "Whew," thought Roger, relieved, as he dumped the 15-page proposal on the floor. Good riddance. By the meeting's end, the discarded proposals covered the floor.

"See Roger. You're smarter than you thought," said Ricardo, who suddenly appeared next to him, which gave Roger renewed courage.

After lunch the panelists began reviewing a proposal on cell division in beetles.

"This proposal is a fishing expedition and totally unrealistic," exclaimed Dr. Howard Struther, who was from a prestigious Ivy League university. Several people nodded knowingly, and everyone looked very somber. Struther was a heavyweight, a senior, celebrated scientist. He wasn't the type easily contradicted.

"I agree," piped in Dr. Leon McCarthy of Longwood State University in Nebraska.

Dr. Struther continued. "First, there is no evidence that retinoblastoma protein has anything to do with regulating the division of the stomach cells of this creature, so why look for proteins that interact with it after the animal has been fed? Moreover, the genetics of beetles is in its infancy. Few mutants are available. In fact, I'm not sure of any that are known. Also, Blalock – is that the Principal Investigator's name? – yes, Blalock. He doesn't have a good environment to do that kind of work. Jones College – or is it Jans College? – is an undergraduate institution."

The second reviewer of this grant, Dr. Jennifer Skidmore, an ambitious and clever Assistant Professor at another Ivy League university, agreed wholeheartedly with the compelling Dr. Struther. "Absolutely," she said. "Agreed." Her horn-rimmed glasses rested snugly on the bridge of her nose and shielded the fire in her eyes, which matched the color of her light brown, cautiously revealing sweater.

Roger thought that she had a bright future ahead of her. She knew when to step aside and when not to. Youth is a wonderful thing, especially when it belongs to the right person at the right place at the right time.

Blalock's proposal was history, just that quickly. Bye-bye Blalock. The rejected proposal was flung onto the growing heaps of completed ones carpeting the floor. The room began to resemble a battlefield.

Roger suddenly saw the messy mounds of rejected proposals as victims treated without compassion, rejects from the inner circle, and he started fuming. His dizzy spell flared up again and he started sweating, as he had just before his outburst in Dr. Thomas's office.

"I'm confused," said Roger, addressing the panel, refusing to give up on Blalock so quickly. "I think that Blalock's proposal should be rediscussed."

He knew that final decisions on proposals were never reconsidered in these instances. Nonetheless, he proceeded. "We approved a request this morning from Princeton that proposed to do essentially the same thing with the fruit fly. Everyone was enthusiastic about it, emphasized that retinoblastoma protein was an interesting regulator of cell division and that there is a great need to find all the proteins with which it interacts. Now Blalock has shown that retinoblastoma protein is present in the stomach cells of a beetle and that there is a burst of cell division in the stomach after feeding. I know, there's much more information on fruit flies than on beetles, and many mutants are known for flies. And Princeton is a research mecca. But doesn't it seem reasonable to study the beetle retinoblastoma protein as well, as Blalock proposes? Comparative biochemistry often yields a lot of information and often reveals surprises and differences. As for Blalock's environment, well, some research *is* conducted at Jones College. Yes, it's Jones College, not Jans College. Blalock has published a few articles in the last two years there, and pretty good ones at that. His proposal may be less advanced than the one on flies, but it's still interesting, and comparison of the role of retinoblastoma protein between the fruit fly and beetle…well…might be interesting."

"I agree," said Ricardo.

Roger wished Ricardo was on the panel.

Dr. Struther looked unfazed. The other panelists seemed restless.

"We are not discussing the beetle proposal anymore, Roger, and we've had two experts agree not to fund the Blalock proposal. You know our policy; once a proposal has been decided we move on. Let's move forward," directed the chairperson. "There are thirty more proposals to go, and they have to be finished by tomorrow noon."

I've had it, Roger thought. Enough is enough! The sweat became a shallow lake flooding his forehead. He couldn't hold it back anymore. The dizziness was turning into a twisting tornado. Perhaps considering all the factors involved in funding a grant proposal did make a case for rejecting Blalock's proposal. Perhaps. But what arrogance of Dr. Struther to discard the grant request because Jones College wasn't up to his standards for a research institution, when in fact research was being conducted there. What justified rejecting a grant request on beetles because less was known about them than about flies? That was too much! And the obsequious behavior of Dr. Skidmore, up and coming Jennifer – preposterous! Wasn't it *more* important to fund research that investigated little-known species than to focus entirely on the projects that added a bit here and a bit there? More would be gained, dollar for dollar, on projects investigating new areas than on those with a plethora of researchers competing with each other on similar projects. Leading projects needed to be well-supported, naturally – that was a no-brainer – but to close the door on a promising young scientist asking interesting questions? NO!

Roger sighed deeply, attempting to quell his inner rage, but his fury ignited his growing anger. Would he accept being part of a panel that pushed Blalock's research aside because it boldly proposed a project on beetles, an obscure species apart from the customary collection of a few, favored, studied species? NO again! He wouldn't stand for that, and the damn broke.

"*You're all a bunch of sheep!*" Roger erupted, red in the face, eyes spitting venom. "*And snobs. What's wrong with Jones College? That it's not Ivy League? What do you know about beetles? Nothing! Are you upset that they won't be front-page news? Is that the problem? That they are not sanctified? That Jones College is minor league, not Ivy League? I've had it!*"

Roger stormed out of the room, leaving his pile of discarded proposals on the floor and those remaining to be reviewed on the table, with his score sheet and half-finished Coca-Cola can looking lonely by the empty chair.

Roger was shaken, but not quite as much as after his outburst with Dr. Thomas. He was getting used to this undisciplined and rude behavior, and it doesn't take long for a few acts to turn unwittingly into a habit. Would they go back to Blalock's proposal and approve it when he was gone? Very unlikely. No, they wouldn't. Yet, he thought that most of the panel members agreed with him although they would never say it out loud. Yes, they *were* sheep. Never mind. Roger felt that his outburst was justified, more so than the one in Dr. Thomas's office, although he didn't expect to be rewarded for his heartfelt explosion, as he had been by Dr. Thomas.

Seldom, however, can the consequence of a sincere act lacking design be predicted, and such would be the case now, once again.

Roger went for a walk while everyone else continued reviewing grants. The weather was divine, a perfect, sunny, 72-degree day, just right for a peaceful stroll. He thought about the Slingshot protein and wondered exactly what that unique protein did to benefit the sponge. So many mysteries to investigate.

Once Roger had calmed down, Ricardo, his faithful apparition, turned up again.

"I couldn't agree with you more, Roger," he said. "And I admire your guts for the outburst, although I'm worried about the consequence. On the other hand, judging from the outcome of the Dr. Thomas outburst, you have a charmed existence.

"And as for mysteries of nature – absolutely! Any thoughts on how jellyfish might see evolution? Damn smart creatures, I'm pretty sure of that. Very sophisticated and highly evolved, as judged by adaptation to its aquatic environment. Did you know that jellyfish produce two vortex rings, donut-shaped bodies of fluid underneath their translucent bodies, that spin in opposite directions to aid in swimming? Each time a jellyfish pulses – squeezes and reopens its gelatinous body – these rings create a type of 'wall' – a 'ground effect' – to push against. Pretty amazing, eh? No wonder these animals have thrived so long. I bet those on your panel wouldn't consider supporting a grant proposal to study how jellyfish swim, unless, of course, someone knows something about water dynamics and engineering and appreciated the biological success of these critters. Which I doubt they know or care about or would support."

Roger smiled. He didn't know that about jellyfish propulsion himself, but he was sure that was only one of many extraordinary secrets yet to be studied further by curious scientists.

That evening several of his colleagues joined him at dinner in the cafeteria and told him that everyone was confused about his behavior. Was he feeling all right? Anything wrong with his health or family? His outburst wasn't like him.

They didn't know of the Dr. Thomas affair.

"I think that Blalock got a rotten deal," Roger said. "What do you guys think? Should Blalock have been rejected?"

"Are you trying to ruin your career? You insulted a whole mess of important people today," said another panel member who joined them for dinner.

"What did the 'important' people say?" Roger asked.

"Funny about that. No one said much except for James. He's a tough chairman, but I think fair. He thought you might need a rest, that you were probably overworked, not to worry, tomorrow is another day. He hoped you would return and, oh yes, that he was always interested in beetles. He went on to the next proposal. *Are* you coming back for tomorrow's session, Roger?"

"Maybe," Roger answered. "Nobody but James said anything at all, and he said that I might be overworked and needed a rest, and that he liked beetles?"

"That's about it."

Roger grinned. He thought that Ricardo would be happy with that reaction, but he didn't make an appearance. Unpredictable, as usual.

The next morning Roger returned, said nothing about his outburst, and finished reviewing the proposals. The Chairman was unexpectedly friendly, and no one questioned him beyond asking if he felt all right. At the conclusion, James Whipple thanked him as he had after previous sessions of the study section.

"You're welcome," answered Roger, still with no mention of his outburst. However, he did say, "I still think Blalock should have been funded."

"Between you and me, you may be right," said James, "but, well, you know, the system works, there are many factors."

"Enough. I get it," said Roger, who did get it, but probably for different reasons.

Before leaving, James told Roger about his ladybug collection – the one beetle that had conquered Roger's heart as well, perhaps because they symbolize good luck. Roger and James discussed briefly the beauty and mystery of beetles.

And, coming from the blue, James said, "I think that you would be an ideal chairman for the next meeting. You're certainly not lacking passion! Can I recommend you to take my place next year? This is my fourth year and I'm finally off, a free man!"

Chairman? Really? Roger pondered. Hmmmm…

"Sure. Thanks, James."

Politics?

Except for Nathan, Roger didn't tell his colleagues about his blowup in the study section. He assumed others would find out via the grapevine anyway.

"It was amazing, Nathan," he said. "Sometimes I think that we are just a set of reflexes triggered by emotions. At least that seems true in my case. Why can't beetles be studied at Jones College? Why do people care so much about flies and not about beetles? Beetles, sponges, they're fascinating. The more we learn about diverse species, the more possibilities we'll have that might benefit us in some way. It just boiled up in me, and I couldn't control the urge to jump off the cliff."

"There you go again, Roger. What were you thinking?"

"Yes, no, I don't know. I wasn't thinking; I was feeling. The more I alienate myself, insult people and stand apart, the more they seem to support me. But I do think I was right. Isn't that important?

"Howard Struther. Pompous guy. Thinks he knows it all. I can't figure out why no one ever challenges him. Is it his credentials or his political power in the science world? I think that Blalock's proposal should have been funded, or at least partially funded, but not totally rejected. I believe most people would agree with that. They're all sheep – bless their wooly souls. But it got Struthered. Anyway, I lost it, for the second time. I thought this time I would really do it, once and for all, draw the line and gallop off past it into the land of prickly plants, commit professional suicide, even though I have no idea what I would do after that."

"Really? But no one seemed especially affected by your so-called tantrum. Looks like your suicide has been postponed, as Mark Twain said that the news of his death had been exaggerated in a premature obituary. Seems to be a pattern with you, Roger. Blast away and get rewarded for it. Insult Dr. Thomas, act kind of nuts and get an award. University Scholar, wasn't that it? Now you'll probably get some kind of award from the Beetle Society of America. If there isn't one, they'll establish one for you. Ha!"

Roger noticed a small cockroach that scuttled in the crack between two filing cabinets in his office as he listened to his friend on the phone.

"Cockroaches are beetles, aren't they," he asked. "Horrible little creatures. Resilient though. They seem to survive everything, even supposedly a nuclear Holocaust."

"What's that got to do with your outburst?"

Roger paused a moment before answering, and then, changing the subject, he told him that James Whistler said he was going to recommend him for next year's chairman of the study section.

"Looks like I'm surviving kind of like a cockroach, Nathan."

"Oh, my god! Really? I can't believe it. I'm going to hire you as my campaign manager."

"Campaign manager? We're talking science, Nathan, not an election."

"Are you sure?" Nathan asked. "You call that science?"

"Well, everything is political," admitted Roger.

"I've got to go teach a class, Roger. Talk to you later. Try not to insult anyone today."

Why not? thought Roger. *It's working.*

A year later Roger accepted to be the Chair of the study section when James Whipple's term expired.

PART II

THE PANDEMIC

Virerium

When Roger was in his mid-fifties, five years after he had finished his stint on the study section, he made a chance finding that brought him international visibility. "Chance finding" didn't mean that anyone could have made the observation. It was more than luck. It was Roger's willingness to go outside the norms of present knowledge and take a chance on looking foolish that led to his insight. It was not only a perceptive biological finding, but it ultimately led to a new perspective of thoughts, politics, art – just about everything – including human nature. In a word, it was *revolutionary*. And it all started with the pandemic.

The insidious disease was caused by a mysterious bug which appeared to have combined the properties of a virus and a bacterium. For lack of a better name, the biological agent was called Virerium, blending the terms "virus" with "bacterium." Since no one ever saw the disease agent, scientists inferred that Virerium entered cells initially, as a virus does, where it captured several key proteins for its replication. After having replicated, the agent traveled to the brain, where it settled in the extracellular spaces, as a bacterium might, and did its damage. Virerium was assumed to be a physical entity, since saliva from a stricken person could infect mice. Yet, while every known microscopic entity connected with life – virus, bacteria, protozoa, even proteins or DNA – had been visualized by some technology, Virerium was defined by only the symptoms of infected individuals. The infectious agent itself remained abstract, a unique infectious 'something'. Scientists speculated that Virerium might be so tiny that existing technology was not capable of revealing its structure. Of course, Virerium could be "something" else entirely. What could that be?

The elusive Virerium represented a new field ripe with mysteries, opening opportunities to learn more about biology, such as, for example, evolution in the absence of genetic mutations or fossils. But it wasn't even known if Virerium had genes, although it seemed likely that it did from what is known about life. If so, were the genes nucleic acids (DNA or RNA, like living forms on Earth), or could they be a different biochemical or new manifestation of life? As for fossils, that was out of the question. How could anyone even look for a fossilized nonentity presumed real by inference from circumstantial evidence? No drug touched the sickness. The only recourse the frightened population had to deal with this menace was patience and hope that it would leave as mysteriously as it came.

Public health specialists had no idea how to deal successfully with the odious disease. It was hard to believe how little progress had occurred to combat a pandemic in general, and only age-old public health measures were employed: stay quarantined at home; wear a mask to protect yourself, wash your hands repeatedly until they were raw, don't touch your face, keep a distance from other people, avoid crowds, try known medicines, whether recommended or not, wait for the development of an approved drug or vaccine, which was impossible since Virerium had never been seen or physically identified. While many victims of the pandemic recovered, many deaths spared no one age-group of people – young, middle-aged, or old. As for those who did die, well, the less compassionate members of society said that everyone dies eventually.

Virerium had a ludicrous side. What fun many cynics had playing with vulnerable minds, as if the pandemic was a yo-yo – up one day, down the next. It was political football. Social media exploded with nonsense, including a theory that it was an attack by aliens from another planet. Politicians were in heaven. Any stupidity they uttered found a receptive audience. Imagine the playground where any argument or idea, positive or negative, was fair game. Do that, or don't do it; try this, or don't try it. Is the absence of facts more or less problematic than false facts? Is inaction more or less dangerous than random action by guesswork? It makes one giddy even to think about it. The dysfunctional government took a fatalistic position: do as little as possible until a vaccine or effective medication is developed, and wait for God, or perhaps God's assistant, to eradicate the pandemic. Ultimately the last option worked, thank God.

Virerium magically disappeared after five years, having reduced the world population by 22%, give or take. Thus, the pandemic – the illness – arrived mysteriously, infected billions of people, remained invisible to science and vanished. No vaccine was ever developed. It was just a horrible happening that announced, "Hello," and five years later said, "Goodbye." No one knew whether or not it would return, or if it would, when? Weird. Terrible. Changed Roger's life. For the better.

Nature remained a collection of mysteries, as always – a few enigmas solved, and the rest not even known to be problems.

Writers compared Virerium to rape by a stranger, who sometimes – rarely – kills the victim and then disappears. This analogy was banned from social media, claiming it was sexist and titillating to sick minds. However, many people posted on social media every type of absurd nonsense they dreamed up, with little concern for its veracity. Psychologists considered Virerium a "living hallucination," a contradictory definition hard to fathom.

Roger thought that "living hallucination" was an apt description of Ricardo.

"Damn right!" agreed Ricardo. "Good term."

Philosophers questioned what was living and what was hallucination? No conclusive answer was agreed upon by everyone. Artists made abstract drawings of what they imagined the mysterious Virerium might look like. Some politicians told the gullible public not to worry, that Virerium was just a bad cold, elect them, they hated colds and would get rid of it. Their rivals said that Virerium would eradicate mankind unless they were elected.

The common man – "Everyman" – trembled with fear. Priests, rabbis, imams, some agnostics, prayed for salvation – any God would do if their favorite one was otherwise disposed. Evangelicals and Hasidim stretched their arms to the heavens and pleaded for mercy. Skeptics suggested that Virerium might be Satan in disguise with the goal of eradicating God's creations. Scientists begged Charles Darwin, not God, to select mankind for survival. They all asked why a merciful God, or any God for that matter, would allow such havoc, suffering and dispassionate, uncaring death. That argument had no punch, since God had allowed even worse atrocities throughout history.

The common mantra was, "We must band together to defeat this treacherous, invisible enemy in our present time of crisis."

Fine, but how would being together defeat the abstract agent?

Roger and Ricardo had different reactions to the pandemic. Ricardo dismissed it and didn't fret since he was dead. He had nothing to lose and could afford being cavalier and told Roger, "Sure, band together as desperate victims, blame God and Satan and even innocent Charles Darwin, and ignore the fact that they sent me to jail for irrelevant research on jellyfish. I don't pity them."

Roger, being a living target for Virerium, was more respectful of the invisible agent. He remained quarantined and followed all the guidelines to remain healthy. It wasn't until the Virerium plague faded out, leaving a gray calm among the survivors, that Roger stepped into the picture.

Diane

Roger made his first insightful observation about the illness when he went for a stroll with Robin on a lovely day after the pandemic had subsided. They had just finished delicious hamburgers, Roger's favorite lunch, although he seldom indulged due to their high cholesterol content. Robin also was a stickler for a healthy diet and made an exception in honor of the first sunny day of Spring. With full bellies, the sky brilliant blue and the flowers budding, Roger and Robin were relaxed and in a good mood.

When they passed the Morgans' house, their 15-year-old daughter, Diane, was playing cards with her friend Judy on the front lawn. They were giggling and teasing Diane's cat, Daisy. It was a happy scene on a happy day.

Diane was inhibited, while Judy was the most popular girl in the class, captain of the cheerleaders and class president. The pair made quite a contrast of characters. Diane often scowled, while Judy always had a welcoming smile and a kind word for everyone. The boys swarmed around her, the girls admired her, and the teachers favored her. Judy was one in a thousand, as they say. To know her was to like her. Not so for Diane.

Roger wondered what gene or genes were responsible for bestowing Judy with such a wonderful personality, which seemed an intrinsic part of her as much as an arm or leg. Judy *thought* pretty.

"Hi there," said Diane, with a big smile when Roger and Robin passed by. "Beautiful day. Good to see you again."

Judy waved hello as well.

Diane was downright friendly. Unexpected. Both Roger and Robin waved back, pleasantly surprised, and said "Hi" in unison.

"Diane, your mother told me a couple of months ago that you had a bad case of Virerium. How are you feeling now?" asked Robin.

"Yeah, it was terrible. I don't think I've ever been so sick in my life."

"But you seem okay. Are you?"

"Yes, perfect. Never better. Thanks for asking."

Roger and Robin waved goodbye and continued their walk.

"Something's weird, Robin. I don't get it," said Roger. "I don't know Diane that well, but she seems different. I can't quite put my finger on it. She was always arrogant and disagreeable, a real pain in the ass, with few, if any, friends. Her mother told me that Judy was Diane's only friend, as strange as that was. I always wondered why such an attractive, obviously intelligent girl like Diane with a loving home environment wouldn't be more friendly and popular at school? And now, suddenly…she couldn't be more pleasant. Weird."

"I agree. She just seemed so…so nice…personable…like she's another person. What the…oh well…better nice than nasty." Robin shook her head, bewildered.

They left it at that and walked on. However, Roger couldn't get Diane out of his mind. She really did seem like a different person. He remembered a run-in with her about six months ago, when her belligerent behavior was in full display. When he had mentioned to her mother that Diane looked unhappy and stressed, she said, "I know. Diane's always like that. I don't know what to do about it. It can be exasperating."

Roger recalled his past experience as he walked silently with Diane. Like today, he had met her on a walk with Robin and retained a detailed memory of that experience since it had impressed him. He recreated the experience in his mind – he relived exactly what Diane was like then – as if it were happening in the present.

Initially he heard a girl's shrill, yet faint, voice in the distance. As he walked ahead with Robin, the sound got louder and was joined by a much lower-pitched calmer voice. After another block, they saw Diane peering up a tree shaking her fist and virtually screaming about something, while Judy stood by trying to mollify her friend. Roger watched the scene with Robin for a few moments from a distance.

"That fucking cat won't come down!" Diane exclaimed. "Get your ass down, Daisy. God damn it!"

"Come on, Diane. All Daisy did was what cats do – they climb trees. Talk nicely and I bet it will come down." Judy was doing her best to get Diane to simmer down.

Diane turned toward Judy with an angry expression on her face.

"Shut up, Judy. It isn't you who will get in trouble. You're always being such a nice person. It gets tiring. Honestly."

"Diane's really nasty," Robin acknowledged. "I don't know why or how Judy stands it."

"You said it. Diane can be horrible. I know it isn't any of our business, but let's try to defuse whatever is going on. Do you want to climb the tree and get Daisy?"

"Are you kidding? That's your job, Roger, if you're nuts."

ROGER'S THOUGHT-PARTICLES

When they got to the girls, Diane was still sniping at Judy, telling her that if she's so smart, why doesn't she get Daisy?

"You're always helping everyone. Little Miss Perfect cheerleader. How do you stand yourself? Get real, Judy."

"Hey, Diane," said Roger, arriving at the scene. "Give it a rest. Why are you so angry? It's Daisy in the tree, not Judy."

Judy hopped up on one branch near the bottom of the tree and said, sweetly, "Here kitty, kitty, kitty. Here Daisy. Please come down. Diane will get in trouble if she goes home and tells her parents that you're up in a tree and won't come down. You wouldn't want that, would you? You're such a nice cat."

Like magic, Daisy purred, scratched her nose with her paw and jumped down.

Roger remembered being amazed. How did Judy do that? What a contrast between the two girls.

"You were just lucky, Judy," said Diane, with no apparent appreciation or thanks for getting her cat back.

Diane hardly looked at Daisy, so Judy picked the cat up, and they left.

Robin broke Roger's daydreaming about the past. "Oops, I forgot that I have an appointment in half an hour and need to go home now."

Roger strolled on for a while enjoying the crisp Spring awakening. About 20 minutes later he met by chance Diane's mother, Dorothy, who also was out catching some sun after a dreary winter.

"Good afternoon. Lovely day, Dorothy. I just saw Diane at your house. She looks completely recovered from Virerium. How's she doing these days, now that her life is normal and she's back in school? She seems happier than ever before." Roger asked.

"Hi Roger. Yeah, Diane's fine. Actually, she's more than fine. I've never seen her so friendly. It's such a relief. She's easygoing for a change, no longer resists her father and me, and has been making friends at school. I can't imagine what caused the change."

"Adolescents do grow up, you know. It sounds like a step forward in maturity," Roger offered as explanation for Diane's change in demeanor.

"Maybe," Dorothy agreed. "But it seems too fast. It's more like a dramatic transformation in her personality. It's so extreme and sudden. If it were a novel or a movie, no one would believe it."

"Could it be simply that she is happy to be well again? She went through quite an ordeal with Virerium."

"She certainly did. It was a rough time."

"How sick was she? Did anything special happen that impressed you?" Roger asked.

"She had muscle aches all over her body, some nausea – the usual malaise of the flu – and a really high, recurrent fever with terrible headaches," Dorothy said.

Dorothy then told Roger about Diane's strange fits – spasms resembling epileptic fits – when the fever rose above 104 degrees. Diane had never had fever that high, and the headaches – they were excruciating. She had remained conscious during the fits and complained of insufferable headaches during these attacks.

"Epileptic fits?"

"I know, it sounds bad. The doctor assured us that she definitely didn't have epilepsy, thank goodness. Anyway, once the fever broke, she stopped having fits."

"Did she complain only about the pain, or was there something else?"

Roger's scientific side slid into gear. Epileptic fits with insufferable headaches while remaining conscious? This was intriguing.

"It was pitiful, Roger. I didn't know how to help her. She shook all over, clutched her head and babbled, '*My brain is taking a shit!*' over and over at the top of her lungs. And *that* could be very loud! Believe me. It was scary. A friend suggested that she was exorcising Satan out of her miserable body, but he's an obsessive Catholic."

Roger didn't pay much attention to that quirky idea of Satan. But the possibility of "something" affecting her brain – a mysterious agent she called *shit*. Was that Virerium? What could it be? Curious. Was Diane's putative brain "shit" something to explore further? It seemed far-fetched, but yet…she seemed so different now.

"I haven't heard about these fits with high fevers and head-aches before, Dorothy," Roger said. "But I'm glad she's okay and happy. She looks great, and friendlier than I've ever seen her. What good news!"

And then they went off in their separate directions.

Roger couldn't stop thinking about Diane's change in personality, and he told Robin about her fits and painful headaches. Robin was more skeptical than he was, which was not uncommon: her sober assessment of circumstances often kept his imagination from going astray. She suggested that what Dorothy interpreted as a change in Diane's personality might be, at least to some extent, a projection of her relief for Diane's complete recovery from Virerium. Or maybe Dorothy was exaggerating. Robin had never found Diane as difficult as either Dorothy or Roger had, and she decided to call Dorothy to check for herself.

"I don't get it, Robin," said Dorothy on the phone, con-firming what Roger had told her. "Diane has become so easy to deal with, so friendly and accommodating since she has recov-ered. What happened?"

"That's wonderful. Do you think it's possible that she, and you, may also be ecstatic that she got well? It must have been so frightening. What do you think?" Robin asked, probing like Roger had.

"No, I don't think so, Robin. Diane's really different – with herself, with me, at school with her friends – even with Judy."

"How so with Judy? What's she got to do with Diane's changing personality?" Robin's curiosity had just jumped up a notch.

After an extended pause, Dorothy said, "I don't know why Judy stayed friends with Diane, considering all the abuse that Diane gave her for no apparent reason. I was embarrassed by it. Judy just has such a kind and lovable personality. But since Diane has recovered, she's sweet as sweet can be with Judy. Now they seem like real friends. It's wonderful. I love to see that."

"Did Judy ever catch Virerium?" asked Robin.

"No," Dorothy said.

"Hmmm…I wonder…"

When Robin told Roger about her conversation with Dorothy, they agreed that something significant had happened to Diane, that she had undergone a monumental transformation, as if a surface layer of her brain – the so-called "shit," – perhaps her unpleasant pre-pandemic personality – was excreted.

Maybe this excreted "shit" – whatever that was – uncovered a layer beneath that led to a more congenial personality. That was a rather wild hypothesis, but how to account for the radical transformation? Yet, it was still unclear just how much Diane's personality had changed. They both wanted to see her for themselves. How friendly had she actually become?

"What do you think, Robin, let's invite Diane and her parents over for tea and cookies some afternoon. That would be a neighborly thing to do, and it would give us a chance to see Diane for ourselves."

"Okay," she said. "I know it's not exactly our business to mix into their affairs, but the situation is…I don't know…strange, and I'm curious."

The following Saturday they got together with Diane and her parents, and they talked about this and that – small talk. Roger made it a point to focus on Diane.

"Diane, I hear you're making a lot of friends lately," Roger said.

"For sure. I went to a party with a group of girls last Saturday," she answered, with an open smile. A glow replaced a previous scowl. Diane was indeed different.

"All girls?" Roger asked.

Diane reddened and said, "Pretty much… well…there was this guy…Tom. He was very…I liked him."

Roger asked her about school. What were her favorite subjects, was Judy still helping her in math?

"A little," she said. "But I'm okay with math now," she added. "Judy's my best friend and we're doing a lot of stuff together. We're going bird watching next weekend."

They went on like this for some time. Diane said she planned to try out to be a cheerleader at the football games, a job she shunned before the pandemic, and that Judy was going to teach her how to do it. Diane couldn't have been more pleasant, and she clearly enjoyed socializing. Her parents were radiant, as if they had just been given a gift of a new daughter. Roger and Robin both found Diane changed from how they remembered her; now she was easygoing and friendly.

It was incredible.

As surprising as this personality transformation was, it might have had a straightforward explanation. Robin still thought that maybe the trauma of Virerium jolted Diane to mature a bit and be more appreciative of good health. After all, it was pretty tough to weather that storm, and Diane was only 15. Teenagers go through many "ups and downs", especially when they discover the opposite sex, which appeared she had – there was Tom. She was probably in a "down" phase before she got sick, and she could have just bumped up into a happy phase for any number of reasons. Perhaps she realized friends were critical for popularity, and so she made a conscious decision to be more social. Also, a little success breeds more of the same. Maybe Diane experienced a series of small satisfactions that grew into an avalanche of success, and it showed in her mood.

"You're right, Robin. There are many possible explanations for teenage mood shifts, new projects, all that stuff. Normally, I'd forget about it. Anyway, Diane isn't our responsibility. But... she's *really* different. I wonder if it will last."

"You truly think there's something interesting here Roger? Like what? Remember, you're talking about a real person, not some character you plan to write about in a short story."

As silly as that last comment was, it made Roger hesitate. His mind had the tendency to roll over from science and fact to fiction and fantasy, and Robin knew it. Thank goodness for her! Yet...

"I'm just curious, that's all. Sometimes science presents itself as a hunch, or even as an idea for a story of some kind – a science story about nature. There's been a lot of science fiction that evolved into real science. What about computers and robots before they existed? Talking and responsive machines? Ridiculous at first. Until they weren't."

"So, what do you imagine, Roger? What's your short story that might turn into science?"

Not having an immediate idea, Roger said the first thing that came to mind.

"Okay, Robin, what do you think of this idea? Diane gets Virerium, fever rages and affects her brain. She has horrible headaches and complains that shit is leaving her brain. Hmmm, what then? Well, maybe shit isn't leaving her brain at all. Maybe something is entering her brain."

"Like what?"

"Like some kind of infectious particle or chemical substance. Something. I can't think of everything at the same time."

Robin looked less skeptical and seemed curious. She nodded for him to go on.

"Maybe that something is like a virus that's in the air. That's it! Diane gets infected with another virus that gets into her brain and, presto, she changes her personality."

"Pretty far out, Roger. How does a virus, or mysterious infectious particle, cause this magic transformation?"

Roger looked down and concentrated as if this was a serious question and the answer would have consequences. As he was thinking, Ricardo appeared, grinning.

"Okay, Roger baby. You put your foot in your mouth this time. But I sympathize. I did the same thing interpreting jellyfish and came up with this fantastic theory that they have brains, see evolution, yadda, yadda, yadda. You know the story. And you know where it got me."

Then Ricardo winked, chuckled, and said, "Let's see you get out of this mess. Infections that change personalities! Right on!"

"You want to know how the virus/particle/chemical, whatever it is, changes Diane, right, Robin?" Roger asked.

"Right."

"Okay," Roger wasn't going to let these skeptics get the better of him. He took the bait.

"Diane's infected with whatever it is, and it carries a thought, maybe in the form of a gene, or maybe something else, but it's ultimately…a *thought*. Yes, that's it. And that thought is very powerful and could have widespread consequences, so let's call it a Thought with an uppercase T to elevate its significance, as long as I'm just rambling on."

"But Roger, we're talking about personality, not a gene. Remember that disaster with an Imagination gene?"

"Really?" responded Roger. "You don't think that personality, or behavior, is affected by genes? What about the possibility that whatever got into her brain activated a series of genes that are responsible for personality? The important thing is that Diane was weak from Virerium, which made her susceptible to this airborne something, which is actually a Thought in disguise, don't forget the uppercase T. That Thought could have initiated changes in gene expression or other metabolic processes resulting in a personality transformation."

"I think you might have a novel there, but a scientific explanation? I don't know." Robin didn't like to wander too far astray.

"I don't know either," admitted Ricardo. "But I sort of like it." And he disappeared, quickly, with no goodbye.

Roger half-smiled at Robin and said he wasn't convinced of his theory either. But then, he liked the idea of having a completely different thought. Something new. Acquiring infectious Thoughts. That was new.

"Not bad," he mumbled to himself.

Robin kissed his cheek. He hugged her in return, and they decided to polish off the uneaten cookies and tea.

Thought Acquisitions

Roger, the perennial scientist, reasoned that if Diane's personality switch was due to a new phenomenon, and if it was connected in some way to Virerium infection, there should be other recovered patients who also exhibited a transformation of one sort or another. He contacted friends and acquaintances whom they knew in the vicinity who had recovered from Virerium, and then he went to see those willing to be questioned. Roger was looking for any type of changes they might have noticed – in personality, opinions, thoughts, anything at all – that might be connected in some way to their illness. If they had experienced any change, he wanted to know how high their temperatures had reached when they were ill, and whether they had had fits and headaches like Diane had. He asked whether her notion of the brain taking a "shit", Diane's term, made any sense to them.

Some people said they hadn't noticed any difference between their mental state pre- and post-sickness, except fatigue for several weeks during their convalescence. They found it odd that he should think that there would have been a change. Most said that their top fevers were somewhere between 102 and 103 degrees, which was unpleasant, but less than the 104 degrees that Diane had. They complained of headaches but nothing excruciating or worthy of note, in their opinions, and seemed to have had a milder form of the disease. Roger let it go at that and sought other survivors of the disease.

A significant segment of recovered patients he interviewed had suffered severe cases of Virerium, in which fevers reached or exceeded 104 degrees. All had extremely painful headaches. A few individuals experienced fits similar to Diane's. It was these individuals that Roger found most interesting. He found a number of them did experience differences of one type or another in what they thought before they were sick. He identified the different cases in his notes by numbers rather than names to retain confidentiality.

"Like what?" Roger asked #3, who mentioned a surprising switch in himself.

"I used to hate canned tuna fish, and now I love it."

Roger didn't think liking or disliking canned tuna fish was significant. Maybe #3 had never given tuna fish a fair chance after he didn't like it the first time as a kid. Or maybe Virerium had affected his taste buds in some way. Big deal. What's taste got to do with personality anyway?

"Interesting," said Roger. "But did you notice changes in anything else?"

"No. I still love chocolate best!"

"Me too," said Roger.

Roger thanked him for his time but didn't think it was worth pursuing. It didn't seem relevant to Diane's personality transformation. Taste for foods and personalities were different categories. He didn't want to twist facts or stretch any interpretation into the sphere of science fiction, as Robin had warned him not to do. However, Roger did find that a number of recovered patients had changed their thoughts or opinions from before they were ill in ways that resonated with Diane's case.

For example, #5, a gentleman in his seventies, was intriguing. Roger first asked how virulent his bout with Virerium had been. His wife, who wouldn't leave his side, fought tears and answered for her husband.

"Oh, my goodness, it was terrible, so terrible," she said. "I thought I'd lost him, you know. He was delirious for days, such a brave sweetie. His fever went up to 105 degrees, maybe higher, I don't know, and he was screaming, yes, *screaming* that his head was about to explode, that his brains were going to splatter all over – he always had more imagination than sense, you know – but oh, my god, my god, I've never seen anything like it. He was having fits too, shaking all over. The poor honeybun. He's not young anymore, you know, no spring chicken, you know, not anymore. Neither am I. You know."

Roger listened patiently and tried to console her.

"There, there," he said. "He's fine now."

Eventually she settled down, took her husband's hand, stroked it once or twice.

"Tell him you're better, sweetie," she said, now under control.

"I'm better," he said, as instructed. "Actually, I'm fine now, feel fit as a fiddle. I never did understand that comparison. Fiddles don't feel. Oh, well. It's just a saying."

"I'm certainly glad you feel well again, sir," Roger said. "Tell me, have you noted any difference in your thoughts or opinions, since you've recovered from that terrible ordeal?"

"Oh, I can tell you that…" his wife piped in, starting to answer the question.

"Please, I'd like to hear it from him," said Roger. "He might use a word or a phrase that could be important."

His wife pouted, removed her hand from her husband's, and said, "Go ahead, honey. Tell the man what he wants to hear."

"It's been a shock, Roger. May I call you that?"

"Please do."

"Okay. I'm a Democrat, as were my parents. I've always been a Democrat. I'd never considered being anything else than a Democrat."

"He gets the point dear. Go ahead, tell him the rest," said his wife.

"Since I've recovered from that damn disease, I started being swayed by Republicans. Isn't that unusual? Now I actually think they are more correct than the Democrats much of the time. I'm going to vote for the Republican. Can you believe it? That'll be a first for me."

Wow, Roger thought. What caused that? And then, without further questioning, his wife registered her views again.

"Finally," she said. "It took him forty years to see the light of day. I've been trying to convince him for our whole marriage that Republicans are right. Taxes are too high, the government meddles with everything in our lives, but...anyway, it's a... mindset."

Mindset! That's it. Mindset, a complicated concept for thoughts, just as personality is a complicated concept for behavior.

Roger was thinking a mile a minute.

He interviewed a host of other individuals who had recovered from Virerium. Many of them had radical changes in thoughts and opinions, which reminded him of Diane's personality switch and the older gentleman's political transformation. It's fair to note that there were almost an equal number of people who had not experienced any change.

A father, #15, said that his friends had complained that he lacked a sense of humor and essentially never laughed or told a joke. After he recovered from Virerium he loved comedies – movies, plays, entertainers – that he never had cared for before.

Now he laughed. Yes, a lot. And he loved it. The world became funny, and he was a happier man.

Case #19 involved a pharmacist who had become indifferent to his stamp-collecting hobby. Weird, he said, he had loved collecting stamps, but at least his wife was happy because she always resented him spending so much time and money on the stamps.

Roger found many additional cases of thought or opinion changes in persons who had recovered from Virerium disease. He made a list of these and stopped after 47 cases. Enough was enough. Individually, it's doubtful that any of these cases would be noteworthy. Taken together, on the other hand, was another story.

Roger became obsessed with the problem, which latched onto his brain like a pit bull.

Ricardo's Challenge

The interviews opened a Pandora's box of mysteries. Roger believed that he was witnessing some new principle in thinking, which had the ability to alter thought or opinion, or even personality. He wasn't about to let these transformations go without further investigation. Roger was cautiously optimistic that his observations might ultimately lead to new ideas about the nature and transfer of thoughts. What could be more important than that?

As Roger relaxed in his comfortable armchair one afternoon, sipping a cup of coffee and thinking about how to proceed with his investigation, Ricardo made his appearance.

"Hi there, Roger," he said, looking relaxed himself, consistent with his non-matching socks. He was on a social visit, just being friendly, wanting to banter about all the strange data Roger had collected.

Standing in the middle of the room, he said, "I recognize myself in you. I guess blood is thicker than water after all. We're a few generations apart – so what? The distance is no more than a stone's throw across a shallow creek. A million years is a rule of thumb for how long it takes to evolve a new species from its direct ancestor. We have some time yet before that's reached!" And then he smiled in a self-satisfied fashion. He could be annoying.

"What do you mean, that I'm like you? Hardly," Roger answered, although secretly he was very happy that Ricardo, his hero, saw himself in him. "Sit down and let's chat. It's been a while."

Ricardo sat and had the audacity to lean back and put his feet up on the desk.

"Well, your questions are like air, they're like taking a breath for you. Fine, good for you, but you're asking questions about all this 'thought stuff,' which are as impossible to answer as they are to define," Ricardo said smugly. "You're a question-machine looking for concrete answers to abstractions. There's a world of difference between a nerve firing and a thought, just like the huge chasm between the abstract figures I saw on a computer screen generated from a jellyfish eye and the suggestion that jellyfish see evolution. I fought a losing battle, Roger, and now you're doing the same thing. Don't you agree? We ask questions too complex, too embodying other questions within questions, too vague to answer. What's a thought? Come on! Do jellyfish see evolution? We should be writing poems about the absurd."

"You think our research projects are poetic nonsense?" Roger asked.

"Wouldn't you agree that it would be hard for me to prove that jellyfish have brains and personalities and see evolution, or for you to determine how a sick person could suddenly acquire foreign thoughts or, for heaven's sake, a new personality or a different viewpoint on something important to him or her, just like that – wham bam. That's...I don't know. Fuzzy? Imaginative? Magic? Sorry. You're in the same muck as I was in trying to convince the revered inner circle of the scientific community of the validity of my research. It's hard – essentially impossible – to solve a problem that's defined by an abstract question."

Roger scowled, taking Ricardo's statement personally, a criticism for doing unanswerable research on ill-defined abstractions. Yet, Roger knew from years of experience in basic research that Ricardo was right in a general sense: every question was embedded in other questions, creating a labyrinth with no starting gate or finish line, and he didn't have a key to enter the labyrinth, and no idea which way to travel if he had entered. It was the same for Ricardo in his day.

He was right: they were both in the muck.

Ricardo, persistent as always, wasn't through. "Don't be naïve, Roger. I don't mean that we've chosen similar problems. Specific topics don't define us. It's our approach, our *mindset*. Like it or not, I think we – you and me – are drawn to the enigma more than to the solution. Answers, in a strange way, can diminish the beautiful, mysterious question. We may be more humanists than scientists."

Taken aback, suddenly in a déjà vu world, Roger's mind returned to when his teaching assistant in college said that maybe he should major in literature rather than science. He was perplexed: couldn't a scientist be a humanist too? Did a person's mindset, as Ricardo called it, have to be either dispassionately analytical as a scientist or romantically inclined like a humanist? Either/or? Why not both? Wasn't a scientist a human?

Ricardo continued.

"Do you remember how, when I was interrogated during the trial in which I was indicted for spending federal funds on irresponsible and irrelevant research – that really hurt, by the way – I was asked how I justified my jellyfish research?"

"I read your biography, but don't remember that. What did you say, Ricardo?"

"I said I was seeking questions, not answers. I didn't have a fixed destination in mind or a specific problem to solve. I was a reverse scientist in the sense that I didn't provide solutions. I generated problems."

"Yes, I remember. I loved that. You stood science on its head! You were creating problems with all your questions, not solving anything. Terrific!"

"See what I mean, Roger? You're the same. Don't go overboard. I wanted desperately to prove my ideas, but I failed to do so. And I was pissed big time at the prosecutor, such a jerk. He was trying to teach me about basic research. Ridiculous. What did he know? Not much. I couldn't resist toying with him to some extent, which wasn't such a bright idea. Look where it got me. But I really did think that my questions were true progress in knowledge. Questions are always a step forward, even if they are not the right ones to ask, or if forward may mean sideways. Questions open doors to new universes. Questions are key. Without them, there are no answers."

Roger wondered what Ricardo was trying to tell him – that he shouldn't feel bad about not being able to answer the questions raised about thoughts, that the questions were enough, that he should be happy to settle for those? Ricardo meant well. However, Roger believed, the questions gave some structure to the nature of thoughts. The answers were important. Questions without answers of some sort weren't helpful.

Roger wanted to understand the mysteries before him, he wanted to put another notch on the stick. He wanted answers.

"Sorry about all your problems, Ricardo," he said. "But I *am* going to figure out where the new thoughts of the Virerium patients come from. I'm not abandoning my questions in a stew of other questions. I'm seeing something new. Isn't that the path of progress: observation at the starting gate, confusion along the way, reprieve by intuition, temporary support by optimism, hard work, fleeting euphoria, occasional despondency punctuated with a manic moment or two, and then, finally, hopefully, a splash of good luck? Whew! I feel lucky."

"Holy shit, Roger! That was some outburst. Can I quote you?"

Roger ignored Ricardo's interruption.

"There's an explanation to these thought acquisitions and switches, Ricardo, there has to be, and I'll find it. Don't count me out because you ended up in prison. People having thoughts isn't the same as jellyfish having a brain and seeing evolution. The former happens, people think; jellyfish seeing evolution… wishful thinking. Your failure isn't going to doom my success just because I'm your relative. If you had succeeded, does that mean I would succeed too? No! I'm not you. I can't inherit failure, just as I can't inherit success. Just wait," Roger said defiantly, and then turned to look Ricardo in the eye, to let him know who was boss.

But Ricardo wasn't in sight anymore. Roger was alone in the room.

PART III

THINKING

Hard-Wired or Environmental?

Nathan suggested that Roger should have been a psychologist. While that may have been said in jest, Roger thought that it would be useful for him to hear different points of view regarding the generation and transmission of thoughts. Psychologists didn't worry about the act – the behavior – as much as about the thinking behind the act. Roger consulted a couple of psychologists hoping to gain further insights into what he had observed.

Roger believed that diversity – a scattering of ideas – would bring questions wrapped in more questions, but it would also spawn new ideas to pursue. Some time ago, he had discussed this viewpoint with Ricardo, who stated his agreement by an analogy: knowledge advanced like pellets scattered by a shotgun, he had said, not like a bullet shot from a revolver and traveling in a straight line. And yes, those pellets would create a plethora of possibilities to explore.

When Roger was sucked into an intellectual challenge, he couldn't back away. His persistence often crossed the thin line between constructive tenacity and vain stubbornness. His present challenge attracted him like a magnet attracts metal. He also accepted that the risk – even the probability – of failure was part of the game. He reacted from his gut, without insisting on an ultimate answer. Opening new approaches justified the effort. If all he contributed would be new questions, so be it.

He consulted two psychologists, both friends, for their opinions on the derivation of thoughts – a forensic psychologist who was an expert on the criminal mind, and a Freudian psychoanalyst who focused on the unconscious.

The forensic psychologist had interviewed dozens of individuals who had committed crimes ranging from petty theft to first-degree murder. That led to his believing that certain individuals are born to become criminals. He said, "Thinking followed by behavior – a criminal mind – is genetic, inborn, hard-wired in the character. Criminals of all types have similar thought patterns and similar vulnerabilities and always blame others for their own illegal acts. Criminals of any ilk think alike. It's as if they had swallowed a common criminal pill."

Ricardo, always eavesdropping, popped up again. "How would you answer that, Roger? How do you transfer opinions that are generated genetically?"

"You again, Ricardo? Don't rush me. I'm waiting to draw any conclusions until I think I have sufficient information. Come back later, if you must."

Ricardo backed off, while Roger considered what the psychologist said: that criminality was a way of *thinking* rather than of behavior, and the thinking was like taking a *pill*, a medication, a substance, in brief, a particle of some sort. How curious.

"What's new about that?" asked Ricardo, who couldn't keep quiet. "Everyone knows that drugs induce thoughts of all types, including hallucinations. You could say that I was one! But what about the transmission of thoughts, which are buried in the brain? You can't transfer a brain."

"True," said Roger.

Roger was puzzled. If thoughts are hard-wired genetically, as the psychologist said, how would they be transferred without words, as seemed to be the case in Roger's observations.

Ricardo was right: you can't transfer a brain.

The Freudian psychoanalyst, by contrast, said thoughts are generated from personal experiences, implying parents, teachers, friends, colleagues – in short, the environment.

"What good are all these opinions," Ricardo asked, sitting in the corner, "when the experts contradict one another. The forensic guy says thoughts are inborn, and the psychoanalyst says thoughts come from the outside. Use your own head, Roger. Who do you believe?"

Roger understood that their viewpoints were contradictory. Nevertheless, he needed to know the range of ideas that existed. Due diligence was a pain and often confusing, like now. But still…Ricardo could be so arrogant, suggesting not even to listen to anyone else.

The psychoanalyst continued.

"A person raised in a vacuum wouldn't have any thoughts," the psychoanalyst said, but she didn't sound convinced.

Ricardo wasn't convinced either and asked, "How would you test that idea? Has anyone ever been raised in a vacuum, meaning without any social environment?"

Good question, Roger thought, and he pressed the psychoanalyst for an example of someone raised in a vacuum. Did she know of such a case?

"Perhaps David Vetter, the 'bubble-boy,'" she said. "He was raised in a germ-free bubble since he had severe combined immune deficiency. Exposure to any pathogen could be fatal for him. He didn't have much going on in his environment."

"Nonsense," Ricardo muttered in Roger's ear. "David had relationships with his parents and sister and doctors and nurses.

Also, he spent some time at home before he died of lymphoma at the age of 12. That's hardly an example of being raised in a thought-free environment. Poor kid."

Ricardo was a fund of knowledge.

Yes, Roger thought. No one can live in the total absence of an environment. Perhaps genes are necessary for thoughts in the same way that fuel is required for a motor to function. Hmmm… he thought. "Could the environment be the fuel for generating thoughts – or maybe the genes were the fuel – that stole the thoughts from the environment? How would that work?

"Do you know of better examples of life in a limited social environment?" Roger asked the psychoanalyst.

"I don't know about better examples," she said, "but I can suggest different ones."

She brought up feral children raised entirely by animals – dogs, wolves, monkeys, chickens – a veritable zoo of abandoned or abused children in such situations, starting at a few years of age until being discovered much later, depending on the case. Roger was intrigued.

"These are fascinating situations," she said. "The kids bark or cluck or gesticulate – communicate by whatever 'language' they're exposed to. They crawl around and behave like their animal families, although I admit, it's impossible to communicate with them in their language, so who knows what's in their mind?"

"What do you think, Ricardo?" Roger was anxious to hear his opinion this time.

Ricardo looked pleased to be consulted for a change rather than always interrupting to give his opinion.

"This gets interesting," said Ricardo. "I agree that anyone bombarded by someone else's opinion, like a Virerium patient in close contact with a family member, friend or caretaker, could adopt their thoughts or views. But who convinced Diane to change her personality so completely and so rapidly, or what about the guy who suddenly developed a sense of humor? How does the environment explain either of those? Something's missing."

Ricardo was finally being reasonable.

Roger agreed. The environment would no doubt be consistent with the transformations, but...what else?

The psychoanalyst returned to the question of whether thoughts come from the environment with a new approach, that of ancestry – or lineages.

"Except for immigrants beginning anew, advancing generations of many families follow the footsteps of their predecessors," she said. "A Japanese man told me once that he was the most recent ophthalmologist in his lineage comprising a long chain of ophthalmologists going back some hundred years! That's an extreme, but it was true. I know the guy."

Was she kidding? 100 years? "When did ophthalmology become a separate discipline?" Roger asked.

"Oh, my god. The history of eye diseases and vision is very, very old. It started about 1550 BC in Egypt, and then there was Aristotle, and on and on. Vision has always been a fascination, and blindness was always feared."

She continued. "In another lineage, a lawyer friend of mine displayed a long line of lawyers in his lineage as rungs of a symbolic ladder. There are many such examples. It's common that thoughts, opinions, careers are handed down for generations. The environment programs the thoughts and outlooks and acts as the medium for their transmission. I'm quite convinced of that."

"Maybe," said Ricardo, although no one had consulted him. "But, then again, generations of a lineage share genes. Don't forget, Roger, you've got some of my genes. Perhaps I should give you my condolences. Wouldn't my genes have some influence on who you are and how you think or respond to the environment? See what I mean? Every question ends up by asking another question. It gets tiring."

Ricardo didn't wait for Roger's response. He just did his customary disappearing act – poof – gone.

Roger also knew family lineages in which the generations walked in each other's footsteps – musicians, bankers, athletes. Was that strictly a matter of exposure or convenience or financial stability, or did genetic inheritance play a role?

Roger decided to take a look at his own family tree.

Juliette and Beatrice

Five generations before Roger, Ricardo was too distant to have been a direct influence on him. Nonetheless, Ricardo's bent for science and mix of scientific and artistic sides were strikingly similar to Roger's talents and character, consistent with a common genetic influence. Comparing genes within a five-generation gap is reasonable from an evolutionary point of view. But what about the intervening relatives of Roger's lineage? To what extent did they walk in the footsteps of their predecessors?

Juliette, Ricardo's daughter, posed the most interesting and baffling situation. Photographs showed that she had inherited Ricardo's genes for some physical traits – for example, high cheekbones and an earthy complexion. But she didn't have his dark hair. Hers was silk and gold as her mother, Monique's, had been. A PhD cancer researcher in a pharmaceutical company, Juliette had her father's predisposition for science. She was a brilliant scientist absorbed in her research. However, Ricardo couldn't have influenced her to go into science, since she was an illegitimate child who hadn't met him until she was 30. He didn't even know of her existence until then.

Juliette's diary, saved among family heirlooms, indicated that as a young woman she was idealistic, with no materialistic interests or concern for money. In this trait she resembled her father, consistent once again with a genetic influence. He was a typical absent-minded professor, his mind in the clouds preoccupied with his thoughts and experiments most of the time. Her empathy and strong desire to help those in need must have been a gift from her mother, a nurse, who probably set an example of concern for others.

But a rapid and extraordinary transition in her character appeared when Juliette fell in love in her late twenties with Carl Michelson, a successful financial advisor. Her idealism fell by the wayside, and she became driven by the allure of money and quest for wealth.

To be influenced by a new romantic flame was not jaw-dropping; it happens to many young lovers. Often, it's the rule, not the exception. However, it was the abrupt and lasting nature of this transition that impressed Roger. Juliette's diary clearly stated that when she met Carl on February 6, she had an idealistic mindset. Yet, already on February 10, she became obsessed by a desire for money. "What counts in this world is *money, money and money*," she wrote in her diary, emphasizing and underlining money. "That's almost all that people care about. Until now I had no idea that making money defined success, and who doesn't want success? I do!"

Juliette had become a radically different person in four days!

Four days!! The transition wasn't a temporary exuberance; it was a dramatic and permanent switch in thoughts affecting her character. Due to her sudden lust for cash, she resigned from the pharmaceutical company – so much for science research – and became an apprentice in the financial world of a brokerage firm. Juliette married Carl a few months later, but his roving eye for skirts eventually led to divorce, leaving her financially secure to raise their daughter, Rachel, Roger's grandmother.

Roger would get back to Rachel after Juliette.

Roger was stunned when he read in Juliette's diary about this surprising transformation in her character. The striking similarity to the rapid changes in thoughts in the Virerium patients was impossible to miss. Ricardo, as might be expected, especially when it came to his daughter Juliette, enthusiastically chipped in his two-cents worth.

"My god, Roger, don't let go of Juliette!" Ricardo exclaimed. "Her transformation was amazing – amazing! And it happened in the absence of Virerium. Something general is going on. Whatever it is, it's not limited to an effect of the pandemic. Keep Juliette in mind. She's a valuable bit of data for you. My daughter, Juliette. Wow!"

Roger, surprised at Ricardo's extreme emotional reaction said, " Oh, I won't let go of Juliette, Ricardo. Why would you think that I would?"

Ricardo blushed and looked sheepish. "Sorry for the outburst, Roger. It's just that I was as taken by this switch in Juliette as you were. Remember, I only knew my daughter from her one visit to see me in jail, and by then she was already divorced and had Rachel. I never saw Rachel, except for her photograph when she was two years old that Juliette gave me. How I wish I had known my family – my hidden, illegitimate family – the family I had dreamed of having and never even knew I had, until I did find out, too late to appreciate. Don't you wonder what you don't know about your family – immediate and distant relatives, their private thoughts, disappointments, fears, pleasures, what they thought of you? Oh, Roger, I don't think anyone knows very much about anyone else, not even their family or close friends, perhaps especially not their family.

"Oh, the emptiness within the shell of my brain. Why do I only see what I think to look at?"

Roger let Ricardo speak his heart, for he was sympathetic to his great-great-grandfather's disappointments and unfair destiny. He agreed how little he, or anyone, knows in depth or understands others, even one's family. And how could he ever expect to know whether anyone's thoughts or personality had really changed under any circumstance, when every thought or opinion or conflict is covered by layers of hidden complexity and contradictions? Roger was empowered by Ricardo's reaction. It was so sincere. And the astounding switch in Juliette's outlook was too immediate and impossible to ignore. An unknown "something" must have affected her thoughts and behavior.

"Don't conclude anything too early, Roger," Ricardo warned, having recovered his composure. "And don't ignore the sequence of thoughts and events by concentrating entirely on the thoughts themselves."

"What do you mean, Ricardo?"

Ricardo didn't answer, and as suddenly as he had appeared, he disappeared – hit and run – leaving Roger on his own.

What was Ricardo trying to tell him? Did he mean that the *sequence* leading to thought changes – the mechanism for the transfer from brain to brain – is as, or maybe even more, important than the thought itself? In other words, is the thought transferred by itself, or is it attached to some sort of vehicle that carries it from the donor to the receiving brain? Perhaps the vehicle, whatever that is, released the donor's thought, or perhaps the vehicle carried information that activated the genes of the receiver to have that thought. It was back to the pesty question of whether the transferred thought was received entirely from the environment, or was it activated in the receiver by the environment in some way. Who was correct: the forensic psychologist or the psychoanalyst? Or a combination of the two?

Roger turned his attention to Rachel, Juliette's daughter. Juliette was too self-centered to have written much about her daughter, although there were a few comments about her in the diary. It seemed that Rachel was a lovable and community-minded woman. She married the owner of the local drugstore, spent her life in a small town, and didn't seem to have personal ambitions, a goal she met without difficulty. So much for sweet Rachel. But Rachel had a daughter, Beatrice – Roger's mother – who was a different story altogether.

Beatrice had a significant influence on Roger. There was no reason to consider Roger's father – Beatrice's husband – as an influence on Beatrice or him. That rascal skipped town with the runner-up of a local beauty pageant when Roger was an infant. On the other hand, Beatrice, an actor in New York with wide interests, was a formidable and strong personality.

Already when a teenager, Roger had been curious about how his mother was able to adopt different personalities so convincingly in the theater. He remembered having asked her whether she actually felt like the person whose role she was playing, or whether she was pretending. Did she sense that she *was* that person, or did she remain internally as herself? Was her acting strictly make-believe? He wondered how difficult and quick it was for her to cross from being herself to being someone else in her mind? And for how long did she feel like the character she was portraying when the play was over?

"My acting wouldn't be any good if I didn't honestly feel like the character I was imitating," she had said. "If I'm playing a villain, I *am* a villain; if I'm playing a queen, I *am* royalty. The feeling overcomes me quickly and totally. I *think* and *become* the person I'm impersonating."

Ricardo felt compelled to have his say again: "Sounds like René Descartes: 'I think, therefore I am.' No?"

Yes, Roger thought, but Ricardo could be a pain sometimes. Why does he need to complicate things even more by introducing ancient philosophers? He loved to interrupt.

But still, he was smart and got Roger thinking. Thinking was, in fact, identity, as Ricardo and presumably Descartes imagined. Thinking was part of the sequence of who one is. Thinking, acquiring new thoughts, a new personality, even a new identity, are all processes of becoming – the never-ending journey of life. Roger imagined a common thread running through his various observations: everyone was always becoming somebody else while they remained themselves.

"When the play is over," Beatrice had said, "I become myself again. But what a thrill when the act becomes reality, even for a little while. I'm always surprised how readily I can switch from being myself to being someone else and then back to me. Something takes over my mind."

That his mother could adopt a new personality by *thinking* and, importantly, *believing* what she thought, impressed Roger. Believing one's thoughts must be crucial. Most actors in the theater group said they were faking to become their scripted characters, but not Beatrice. Roger often heard her voice in his mind saying, "Authenticity is as important for an actor as for any artist. An actor must change personality like a chameleon changes color – in response to external and internal stimuli, like temperature or a predator or reproductive state, which would be hormonal. There's just something tangible, more than a mirage, that gets inside your brain."

Hmmm, thought Roger. Something tangible gets inside the mind. Really?

His mother's thoughts knew no bounds: she engulfed different ideas constantly. Were all those ideas due to the "something", more tangible than a mirage, infecting her brain? Roger imagined that his exposure to his mother's wide-ranging thoughts – acting, art, authenticity, biology – contributed to his own roaming mind and multiple interests. How had her ability to have a constant flow of new ideas and thoughts related to whatever "something" infected her mind been passed on to him? Perhaps a susceptibility to whatever it was that affected her mindset gave her, and possibly him, access to many thoughts.

And was that distinct "something" that allowed his mother to *become* someone else on stage the same as the "something" that got into the mind of Juliette to transform from idealism to materialism, or the individuals stricken with Virerium to acquire new thoughts and opinions and even personalities?

"Curious," said Ricardo, back again and insisting to have the last word. "But here's a question that you might consider, Roger. What was it about Virerium that seemed to trigger, or at least enhance, the changes in thought and character?"

Once again, Ricardo had raised a key question. Virerium must have created conditions conducive to activating or releasing or receiving the "something" responsible for acquiring new thoughts. It was the sequence of events that Ricardo continued to question. Roger remained clueless as to what that might be, yet he sensed that he was on to something new and important.

He smelled it, he could almost taste it, he wanted to touch it.

What's a Thought?

Roger reviewed his notes and consulted Robin, who was always helpful.

"I've gone over the interviews with the Virerium patients and my family lineage, trying to make sense of it all, Robin. My lineage indicates inheritance of physical traits and predispositions. Genetics is always present, even if it hides its potential for a generation or two before re-expressing itself at later generations. Nothing new there. And then the obvious: thoughts and behavior are affected by the environment, as the psychoanalyst said. It fits with my mother changing her character when she played different roles as an actor, indicating that even a temporary time in a foreign environment, or a willful transformation, can impose conscious changes in behavior and identity. Rachel's behavior, my grandmother, was consistent with the environment in a very low-key way. She had a limited lifestyle that lacked intellectual stimulation, and never outgrew herself. Too bad.

"But Juliette! She underwent a radical and rapid change in thoughts and outlook that were truly unexpected and difficult to explain. Juliette's transformation of thought, personality and even identity, reminded me of the sudden acquisition of thoughts in Virerium patients. I wonder what the link is."

Ricardo made a transient appearance in Roger's mind, smiled and nodded his approval, and left. It was one of the rare occasions in which he came but didn't say anything.

"I don't know where to go from here," said Roger. "Maybe I should write novels instead of doing science. Ricardo thinks I'm more a poet than a scientist. He thinks the same about himself."

"Ricardo again?" Robin seemed annoyed, although she was aware of Roger's fixation on him. "Ricardo's been dead for over a hundred years. Why put your fantasy in a dead man's mouth? Maybe, it's you who wants to be a poet or writer. Didn't you tell me that your teaching assistant in college suggested that you might major in literature rather than science? What would your novel be about?"

Robin knew that wasn't what he wanted, not now anyway. He wanted to know where thoughts came from. Period.

"What should I do?" Roger asked, seeking support rather than advice.

"You mean, should you write a novel or try to figure out why Diane and the others had all those thought changes associated with Virerium?"

"Don't *you* think that Diane's flip-flop was beyond coincidence, as well as the others infected with Virerium, who had such dramatically different thoughts and outlooks after recovery from before they were ill?"

"Yeah, I do," Robin admitted.

"Don't you think it's worth continuing to try and figure out why?"

"Y...e...s," she said, drawing out her answer, and then she hesitated another moment with a worried expression on her face.

"What's wrong, Robin?"

"Umm, nothing. I just don't want to see you getting into trouble. You're out of your expertise with all this. It's like trying to play the clarinet without knowing the fingering. That's all. It almost seems as if you are trying to do science by writing a novel."

Robin could be harsh sometimes. But he wasn't sure what she really thought now. Maybe it didn't matter. She was entitled to her opinion; he to his own.

"I'm careful," Roger answered. "But such radical changes in the thoughts and mindsets of the Virerium patients – that's telling me something. And Juliette's similar massive personality change. Isn't that curious? I want to know how that happened. I have no clue at the moment. It's crazy! Is it even a meaningful scientific question? Ricardo doesn't seem to think it is."

"Ricardo again!" Robin, her mind planted in the present, couldn't understand Roger's obsession with his ancestor Ricardo.

"What do biologists say about thoughts? That seems like an appropriate question for you to ask. After all, you're a biologist."

Roger crunched his brow and squinted with tension in his face. "That's right, Robin. Thanks. What about the hard-core biology of thinking?" he said, half aloud.

Robin was pleased that she might have helped. "Good luck, Roger. I've got stuff to do," and off she went.

After looking up a number of neurobiological articles on cognition and behavior, Roger was overwhelmed. If he understood it correctly, thoughts and memories were neuronal circuits – linked nerve cells – that formed in the free association areas in the frontal lobes of the brain. The circuits also incorporated neurons from elsewhere in the brain, expanding the scope and opportunities for cognition and thinking and linking emotions to thoughts. Roger thought that the circuits in imagination must have been particularly complex. He wondered how the functional connections of neurons creating thoughts were made in the brain when it incorporated new thoughts, which often occurred in a flash.

Computer models also involved circuits programmed to have specific responses or tasks to accomplish. Roger had been aware of this ever since his college days, when he had defended his case for passive learning to the teaching assistant, arguing that computers were an example of the use of programmed information to derive new conclusions. Was this actually like what happened in the brain? Engineering such circuits led to robots responding to commands. Was this similar to establishing thoughts? Did robots think? Were brains computers, and computers a type of brain? Was Diane a robot? Maybe in some ways she was, such as involving brain circuitry. No. It didn't smell right. Diane was a sensitive girl, not a robot.

Roger stepped back from technical aspects of the brain, which were beyond his knowledge base. He next considered brainwashing of war prisoners and the insidious "Big Brother" in George Orwell's *1984*. Could the thought changes in the Virerium patients have any relationship to being brainwashed? Maybe, but who or what was "Big Brother"?

PART IV

THOUGHT-PARTICLES

The Epiphany

One Sunday morning snowflakes drifted down from gray clouds hiding the sun. Roger put on his boots, down jacket, sheepskin hat and wool gloves and went for a walk in the calm atmosphere. Mist obscured his vision, leaving gray space for him to fill with memories, imagination, and dreams, allowing his thoughts to mingle with his feelings as he explored fantasyland. He could be a Wimbledon tennis champion, or a Nobel Laureate, or a criminal with a kind heart, such as a modified Robin Hood, who stole to give to the needy. Or he could think about the generation and transmission of thoughts. His choice.

Roger resurrected people buried in his mind – childhood friends, science colleagues, neighbors – as well as recent acquaintances or imaginary constructs in his mental universe. Despite all these possibilities, Ricardo was always foremost in his mind, waiting patiently to be called. What a privilege to converse with anyone – dead or alive, past or present, make-believe or imagined – without uttering a word out loud. He could say in his thoughts whatever crossed his mind to whomever he pleased, oblivious of caution or error. Sometimes he lectured to an attentive audience to test ideas, sometimes he talked with skeptics to win their approval, sometimes he confronted critics to clarify his thoughts, and sometimes he unleashed an internal monologue to hear his own voice.

As snowflakes landed softly on Roger's face, the sea, a passion for him, came to mind. He imagined the calm blue-green surface, reflecting sunbeams, contrasting with the brilliant blue sky.

"What a privilege to be alive," Roger said out loud.

His mind wandered from that image of a cloudless sky to one of distant clouds advancing slowly towards him. Intermittent wind gusts agitated the sea, now blue-gray, sporting angry whitecaps. Oh, how Roger knew such creeping disturbances and angst, sometimes with cause, sometimes without. When the wind increased to a gale in his mind, swells morphed into monstrous waves that crashed along a rocky shore. Roger had experienced such violent storms within himself – tantrums he couldn't contain – regardless of whatever or whomever was in his path, as precursors to outbursts. At such times, he *was* the angry sea. And like the sea, he became calm again with time, as all cycles follow their circular paths.

Roger also thought how deceptive the sea could be. The colorful displays of flower-like corals and sponges inflicted painful toxins, sometimes deadly if touched. Hazards roamed beneath the surface. He thought of great white sharks, stingrays, poisonous jellyfish, and many more threats, as well as powerful currents, even rip tides at the shore, and hot vents spewing boiling water from the bottom – Nature's amoral rules – all buried mine fields.

Finally, Ricardo appeared by Roger's side. "How beautiful," he said, pulling Roger out of one daydream into another. "How peaceful the falling snow as it floats down."

"I agree, Ricardo. I believe there's nothing better than our time on Earth."

"I know you do. That worries me," said Ricardo.

"Believing there's nothing better worries you? That's... absurd."

Ricardo shook his head. He sucked his lips in between his teeth and looked down at the ground covered with fresh snow.

"Absurd?" Ricardo repeated rhetorically. "Believing can be absurd, certainly, yes, at least I agree. I *believed* I was right about jellyfish having brains and seeing evolution. I still believe it… is that absurd? I observed impartially. I interpreted the data; I didn't force the data or any other facts into my fancy. I had evidence supporting my conclusions and speculations. I spoke the truth, my truth…and ended in jail. Did jellyfish see evolution? I believed they did. But now, I'm not certain. Maybe my interpretations were…ok, absurd, or at least partially absurd."

"And you think I'm deluding myself, confusing belief with proof?" Roger asked.

"The future will decide. You're honest and don't consciously fabricate your truth. You believe with honesty. But, Roger, the sea – life – is choppy. The opaque surface hides great depth. Beware its beauty and temptations. Beware your alluring thoughts and flights of fancy and grandeur, as sincere as they are. Beware the razor-sharp edges of belief. Belief is neither reality nor proof. Destiny is an autonomous beast! Don't emulate me. Destiny follows its own path – maybe better, maybe worse than you hoped. In any case, your destiny will no doubt be different than you might have predicted or had in mind."

Roger stopped short, as if slamming on the brakes of a speeding car, and turned towards Ricardo, but he wasn't there anymore. Such a frustrating guy! Roger felt there was no time to have a serious discussion with him. Up and down. Here and then not.

Ricardo may have left the scene, but he did not leave Roger's mind, which recalled Ricardo's extraordinary epiphany. Ricardo had connected the changing abstract designs on a computer screen generated by electronic signals from an impaled eye in jellyfish and the appearance of different formaldehyde-fixed invertebrates stored in jars on shelves in the laboratory, two distinct observations that didn't seem to have anything to do with one another. Yet, that was the moment when Ricardo had an epiphany that jellyfish saw evolution. It was such an unlikely connection between the similarity of the abstract designs on the computer and the shapes of the fixed invertebrates. Startled by this revelation, Ricardo wrote in his laboratory notes, "*These images change from one to another in a way consistent with the evolutionary pathway of the species that the jellyfish is looking at, suggesting that jellyfish see videos of evolution!!*"

What a leap of faith! Ricardo truly *believed* what he thought was a credible interpretation of his data. But his belief wasn't proof and didn't satisfy the scientific community. He knew that. Many considered his hypothesis outlandish – the product of someone unhinged, or a charlatan – despite his numerous respected achievements and award-winning scientific contributions in the past. Maybe he had become too old for his own good when he investigated jellyfish. Maybe if he hadn't believed so deeply in himself...maybe...

Ricardo's voice echoing in Roger's mind was replaced by his own epiphany, which was far less complex than Ricardo's. His epiphany amounted to one word – *proximity*. He suddenly realized that all the new thoughts and opinions and personality changes that he had observed involved a transfer from one individual physically close by. This was also true for Ricardo's epiphany – he connected jellyfish vision with evolution, a bizarre thought he never would have had if the abstract designs on the computer screen and the bottles of fixed invertebrates on the shelf had not been next to each other, with him in between. Similarly, Roger reasoned, the Virerium patients never would have adopted the foreign thoughts they did if there wasn't a person nearby who had that thought, or personality, or opinion.

"My god," exclaimed Roger. "Holy shit! Of course! It's so obvious! *Proximity.*"

How curious – the simplest idea or observation is often responsible for advancing a creative project to the next step.

Thought-Particles

"Robin, I'm on to something important, finally. It's my first insight. Maybe…it depends on…I'm not sure…"

Roger carried on like that for a while, following his muse, starting but not finishing sentences, expressing muffled optimism and childlike excitement. He hadn't yet fully engaged his brain; that would come later. He wouldn't ramble like that with anyone else but Robin. She understood him, and he depended on her belief in him. Robin knew when to listen.

Roger reminded her about Ricardo's epiphany.

"I know, Roger. You've told me that a thousand times, and I've read *Jellyfish Have Eyes*, twice, in fact."

"Sorry. In any case, as I thought about Ricardo's epiphany, I had my own epiphany. It's simple, but…well, my idea is that – don't laugh – the thought transfers in Virerium patients required…*proximity*. That's about it."

"What? Proximity is an epiphany?"

"I know, you're wondering what's interesting about that? I'm not quite sure yet, but I think it's a step forward. Isn't that the way progress works? An intuition. A small challenge to current dogma. Upsetting the apple cart. By proximity, I mean that thoughts don't have to be abstractions generated internally. Maybe they can have substance and a physical structure. Who has ever imagined a thought having a physical existence, like some kind of particle? That's more than a small step. That's a leap. What if a thought is like a contagious virus? What if people could acquire a thought by infection with a substance – an actual *thought* in the form of a particle? Sounds crazy? A bit, maybe. But to catch that particle, it must be close by, in the vicinity, next to the person it infects passively."

Roger looked at Robin with his soulful brown eyes, pleading for a positive response. He was excited with his new idea – thrilled, in fact – but feeling insecure at the same time. It was...bold...new...imaginative. But was it real or just fantasy? Was it absurd? Was it just another Imagination gene?

"What do you think, Robin?"

Roger relied of her opinions to keep him from wandering too far into fantasy. Hearing his own voice helped him know if he was on the right track or whether there were flaws waving red flags. Speaking was thinking for him, it made him both author and critic wrapped in one. But speaking wasn't reliable; it was too close to be objective. He needed Robin's input even more than he needed Ricardo's opinion or blessing. Anyway, Ricardo seemed to be taking the day off.

"It's baffling, Roger. I don't know. It's...different."

Robin tilted her head to the left and narrowed her eyes, a habit whenever she focused her thoughts trying to understand a new idea, as if to rearrange or energize her brain.

"You really do think that thoughts are like a virus, don't you? Infectious. I don't get it, Roger. What do you mean? Tell me more."

Great, thought Roger, I passed the first test. She didn't laugh, and she's curious.

"Yes, my idea is that thoughts can be independently contagious, like a virus. Not a virus exactly, but like a particle of some type that can be transferred from one person to the next. I haven't quite crystallized what I think yet."

"You mean that the thoughts themselves – words, ideas, opinions, even personalities – are infectious particles? Are you feeling okay, Roger? Any headaches? Fever perhaps? Too much wine lately?"

Roger didn't bother to answer. He let the infectious particle theory sink in and believed the idea had potential.

Suddenly, Roger saw Ricardo's head protruding through the open door. So, he wasn't taking the day off. "Beware of believing yourself too much, Roger. Remember?"

Without belief, what's left, Roger wondered? Why was Ricardo so damn sure of himself all the time? Wasn't his certainty a belief in himself?

"That's right, Robin. I really wonder whether thoughts can be particles. That's my latest theory," Roger said, sneering at Ricardo still in the doorway.

"Ingenious, I guess. Giving substance to abstractions? At least it's original," Robin acknowledged.

Original! Yes, she likes it, Roger thought, and then the dam broke, and he flooded her with his enthusiasm.

"An abstract thought being a particle, a Thought-Particle. I love it! My god, Robin, can you imagine the implications? Thinking by infection, a type of illness, being influenced by your spouse, or a close friend, because of physical *proximity*, not internally generated words. The Virerium recovering patients I spoke to acquired new thoughts from their caretakers or other close individuals. Diane received Judy's personality, the Democrat received Republican thoughts from his wife (poor guy), on and on. The thoughts weren't simply dreamed up out of the blue. They were 'caught' from someone in close contact. The thought transfer was a passive event, a delivery from a messenger. It's like being infected by a virus or bacteria: some people catch it, some don't. Maybe they're immune for some reason. It fits what I've seen with the Virerium patients. The thought transfers were sporadic. They were...Thought-Particles!"

Robin rolled her eyes and said, "Okay Roger, if you say so."

It wasn't as if Robin wasn't paying attention to Roger or thinking about something else or patronizing him. She always took him seriously. She was going along with vintage Roger, as she had so many times. She was skeptical about this strange idea of Thought-Particles, that was true, who wouldn't be about such an unorthodox hypothesis? Thought-Particles. Imagine! But that was Roger: imaginative, eccentric, neurotic at times, such as his obsession with Ricardo. She was giving him space to be Roger. Maybe he was on to something. Maybe not. At least he was always interesting. And, maybe, just maybe...

She wondered what Ricardo might have said to Roger about the idea of Thought-Particles. Did he like the hypothesis?

She was getting curious.

Ground Rules

Roger laid down two ground rules for himself. First, he would not prematurely reject his idea about Thought-Particles, even if it elicited strong criticism. Second, and this was important, the Thought-Particle hypothesis could exist without discrediting one or more other ideas about acquiring thoughts. More than one pathway to achieve a similar end is common in biology. Both birds and insects can fly but they have different wing structures, and both insects and vertebrates evolved structurally different eyes – complex in vertebrates and compound in insects – yet each type has acute vision.

Nature exploits every possibility and selects what works well under the conditions. That doesn't mean that Nature's choice is the only one that works, or even the best one possible. What about adding a few extra eyes around the head to appreciate the wider view and escape predators, or even have a sixth finger with an eye on each hand to be able to search for something that may have rolled under a sofa or in the back of a tree? Nature allows bees, but not humans, to see ultraviolet light. Pondering ideas, letting his mind jump from one to another, for identifying and solving problems always stimulated Roger.

There is even more than one definition of vision. Is it necessary to perceive an image to call it sight, or is a functional response to light intensity also vision? And what about the senses in general – sight, sound, smell, temperature, taste, touch? Nature devised multiple ways to sense the environment, and different species favor different senses. Separate and interacting networks have evolved to modify or enhance the preferred senses.

Therefore, Roger believed that Nature probably evolved multiple ways to transfer thoughts. Thought-Particles may be one way to access thoughts, not the only way. Thinking is too important to limit ways of doing it. Thinking is imagining, creating and surviving. There is no way to outwit evolution, or for evolution to confine itself to one pathway.

Bittersweet as it may be, however, Roger decided that he would relinquish his Thought-Particle hypothesis if he was convinced to do so by compelling evidence against it. He was tenacious, but not stupid.

Roger's greatest vulnerability was fear of looking foolish, a trait he shared with Ricardo. Even the *idea* of being ridiculed infuriated him. No matter how clever or capable he was, he felt the need to prove it continually to be respected or even to prove it to himself. At least Robin hadn't laughed when he told her about his Thought-Particle theory. That was a good sign. Nonetheless, Roger was haunted by Ricardo's sad fate and didn't want to end as he did – deleted from the high echelon of success, an outcast in prison, a poor and foolish scientist.

Oh, the shame of being branded a charlatan for having such an original notion as Thought-Particles, which could appear as absurd as jellyfish seeing evolution.

"Goddamn those idiots!" he exclaimed to the empty room, protesting these imaginary criticisms. "Why would anyone object to any hypothesis that hasn't been disproved? What would they be scared of? Cowards! Why ridicule me because I have the imagination and courage to risk making mistakes or to inhabit obscure ideas? Nothing ventured, nothing gained. Are Thought-Particles the mark of lazy thinking and make no contribution at all? They're solid substance, not abstract air! They exist!!" he shouted, although no one was listening or even present.

That wasn't quite true. Robin heard Roger in the next room, and she came to see what his tantrum was about.

"What's wrong, Roger?" Robin asked, looking concerned.

"Oh, sorry. I didn't mean to disturb you. I can't believe how limited people are and not willing to consider something new."

"Really? What's new? Who is limited?"

Roger was red in the face, his forehead beaded with sweat.

"No one is limited…yet," he said, doing his best to calm down. "Sometimes I get upset for no reason, or maybe prematurely for a reason, in anticipation. But still…you know."

"I know? For no reason? Prematurely? Anticipation?"

Despite her questions, Robin knew, as Roger knew she knew. She knew that outbursts were his protective walls that, strangely, had been a road to success. Hadn't he been rewarded for his outbursts? What about receiving the Outstanding Scholar Award after his outburst with Dr. Thomas, or the chairmanship of the study section after his outburst with James Whistler when evaluating grant proposals? Didn't his colleague Nathan say he could always find the needle in a haystack? Roger's needle seemed to be a prize buried in a haystack of apparent catastrophe. Why shouldn't he give free reign to his temper? His .outbursts were like a tennis player's tantrums – to energize himself when he missed a shot, or even if he hadn't missed, even if he was ahead.

Robin went back to whatever she was doing and Roger, now in control of himself, continued to imagine Thought-Particles.

Mental Telepathy

Roger divided his batch of interviews with recovering Virerium patients into two groups. In one group, the individuals didn't have any new opinions. Their thoughts and beliefs remained the same as before the pandemic, as was the case in the control group of individuals who had not contracted Virerium. In the other group, the interesting one, a major shift in thought or opinion – even in personality – had occurred.

Ricardo's daughter – Roger's great-grandmother – who, according to her diary, had switched suddenly from her previous idealistic outlook to one who put money and greed front and center within four days after falling in love with a financial advisor, especially puzzled Roger. Since the switch occurred before the pandemic existed, the sudden switch didn't require Virerium infection.

Roger considered briefly that these thought transfers might be due to mental telepathy, an unproven pseudoscience or paranormal phenomenon responsible for the transfer of information or feeling from one individual to another. Such a psychic phenomenon, claimed by some to be true, had a long history. A nonprofit organization, The Society for Psychical Research, had been established in 1882 in the United Kingdom to study mental telepathy. Believers swore that it could occur over vast distances, even between individuals in different countries. Roger, however, didn't know any scientists who believed in mental telepathy. He had no evidence for distant transfers, and even if such a phenomenon existed, it didn't fit with his belief that proximity was critical for the thought transfers he had noted.

Roger decided to consult Adam, his colleague with ency-clopedic information about anything to do with science.

Memes

Roger invited Adam and his wife, Lindsay, to his home to pick his brain about thought acquisitions. Robin and Lindsay were friends, so Roger hoped he could go into his study after dinner with Adam and talk without interruption. He told Robin of his intention, and she was fine with it.

After dinner, the two scientists mulled over the cases of thought transfers and Roger's theory of Thought-Particles.

"What do you think, Adam? Pretty amazing, don't you think? Thoughts as particles – does that make any sense to you… or is it…ridiculous?"

"You're going off the deep end again, Roger," Adam said. "Can't you ever ask me a question that might have an answer?"

"I know. Sorry. My friend Ricardo says the same thing."

"Ricardo? Who's he?"

"Just someone I know. About my idea of infectious Thought-Particles. What do you think?"

"I don't know. It's certainly off-the-wall," said Adam.

Adam remained silent as he dipped into his reservoir of knowledge. Roger hoped Ricardo wouldn't appear and create difficulties. He wanted to discuss this quietly with Adam.

"What about memes?" Adam said

"Yeah, I've heard of them, but that was long ago, back in the mid-twentieth century, no? What exactly are they?"

"Memes were dreamed up in the 1970s. A scientist called Richard Dawkins suggested the meme concept in his classic book, *The Selfish Gene*. They were defined as units of thoughts and ideas – packets of a type – that raged through the population and spread like a pandemic. Memes sound to me like the kind of thing you're talking about."

Adam's memory was like a computer.

"Perhaps. I'm not sure." Roger looked concerned, more worried than intrigued.

"I don't know if scientists are still thinking about memes," Adam said. "It seems to me that they are more for sociologists than scientists, but I doubt Dawkins would have agreed with me."

"Probably not," said Ricardo quietly in Roger's ear, as if making sure Roger knew he was there but he didn't want to bring attention to himself this time.

There was no escaping Ricardo, so Roger had no alternative than to accept his presence and make the most of it. At least Ricardo always added perspective on just about everything.

Spurred on by Ricardo's interest, Roger became increasingly concerned that memes were like viral infections, and that struck him forcefully, like a whack on the head. Were Thought-Particles a derivative of what had already been proposed? Were they no more than a new name for a meme? That would undermine his insight of Thought-Particles. Had he been "scooped" in the race for primacy?

"Settle down, Roger," Ricardo whispered behind him. "Don't be so egocentric. Every basic scientist lives in fear of being scooped. Keep a stiff upper lip! Remember, nature doesn't belong to anybody. Do you think that the moon belongs to

Galileo because he saw it up close with a telescope hundreds of years ago?"

Roger feared that Ricardo was preparing him for the worst – that Thought-Particles were memes – big deal – he'd been scooped about 150 years ago. Don't worry about it.

But Roger did worry.

"Memes do sound similar to what you're describing," said Adam.

"Maybe," said Roger. "From your description, memes are transferred from brain to brain, just like Thought-Particles. They are infectious in that sense. But still…I haven't any evidence that Thought-Particles create a kind of "thought pandemic". Isn't that at the heart of memes, almost their definition, that they spread like wildfire?"

"How do you know that Thought-Particles don't? You didn't look for such spread," Adam said.

"Are you kidding? How could I look for a personality change in someone I don't even know?"

"Careful, Roger," Ricardo interceded. "Don't get defensive. Remember, this is a scientific problem, not a personal expression of your daydreams."

"Maybe what you're calling a Thought-Particle is a type of meme," said Adam, "a meme that provides the *ability* to change thoughts or opinions or even personality. Any particular change you find is only one possible manifestation of that ability. Maybe your Thought-Particle is similar to the concept of evolvability for evolution, you know, selection for an increased ability to evolve."

"Man, Adam is a flow of information and knowledge. Better listen carefully, Roger," said Ricardo. "But, I admit, it's getting confusing."

"Evolvability?" Roger repeated, heeding Ricardo's advice. "You mean what I'm calling a Thought-Particle is really some kind of process that enhances the ability to acquire thoughts? No, that doesn't sound right. Anyway, how would you test for an ability like that?"

"I agree. That would be pretty hard," said Adam. "So, you're down on memes, right?"

"I think I am," said Ricardo.

"I suppose so," Roger muttered. Then, with more assurance, he added, "I don't think memes are anything like Thought-Particles. Memes seem like fads or rumors or the latest popular idea or fashion. The Thought-Particles I have in mind don't spread like that. A meme may be infectious by spreading and becoming common knowledge, but it's definitely not a substance. A chemist could never isolate a meme, which is an abstraction, and study its properties. I believe that a chemist will be able to isolate a Thought-Particle someday. Won't that be amazing!"

Roger was gaining confidence rapidly.

Ricardo nodded but didn't say a word. Roger didn't know what Ricardo really thought.

"I imagine Thought-Particles as meat and potatoes on a plate," Roger said, "literally, a substance. The food is the thought and the plate the vehicle that transports the thought, although the Thought-Particle could transfer by itself, I guess, and not need a vehicle. Once the particle gets into a brain, it could start a type of chain reaction, like catalyzing new opinions or even personality changes.

"Adam, think about it. It's an incredible idea! A Thought-Particle converts an abstract thought into a *substance*, a chemical or some kind of physical structure, which I call a *particle* for lack of a better name at this point. I have no idea what that particle is. I only know that it isn't an abstraction."

Roger had convinced himself. He wasn't so sure he had convinced Adam or Ricardo.

"Well, if these thoughts are really distinct particles, you should be able to detect them by electron microscopy or some other high-resolution method," Adam reasoned.

Roger agreed, and he was sure that Ricardo would too, although he had disappeared for the moment. Being able to see a Thought-Particle was a prediction that could be investigated by using every type of high-resolution instrument available or inventing a new one. Viruses are visible particles composed of proteins and nucleic acids organized into a complex structure. If Thought-Particles are virus-like, they should be visible under high enough resolution. So, why have they never been seen? Maybe they're unstable and fall apart easily, so seeing one would be an exceedingly rare event. That might account for easily forgetting thoughts right after you have them, as happened often for Roger and many other people, especially with age. Or if Thought-Particles are that labile it might make them unable to create a pandemic and only infect a near neighbor.

Roger rationalized that the putative Virerium virus had also escaped visualization, yet no one seriously doubted that the pandemic was caused by a physical agent that was particulate. Negative evidence – not finding what's expected – doesn't mean it didn't exist. The culprit could escape detection by hiding in a discrete corner in the brain, or it might be too small to see at the highest resolution available, or it might be in such low frequency that it's hard to find. Like a needle in a haystack. There were lots of possibilities.

What a mystery! Was Roger reaching out too far on a fragile limb by proposing that a speculative, invisible particle accounted for thoughts, or at least some thoughts? Maybe. Probably. He knew that a funding agency would say he was drifting in the dark and consider Thought-Particles a "fishing expedition," that much-used reproach of a research project lacking specificity or preliminary evidence, as it was dubbed, and not worth funding. Grant proposals ear-marked a "fishing expedition" always accumulated in the pile of rejections in a study section.

Well, thought Roger, if Thought-Proposals were branded as a "fishing expedition," so what? How else to catch a fish?

Suddenly, Ricardo's voice blasting in Roger's ear. "Don't go into one of your tantrums again, Roger. There's nothing to gain at the moment. There's no prize to be awarded for an outburst now. No one is criticizing you or your idea of Thought-Particles."

Roger saw Ricardo in the back of the room.

Calmer now, Roger hoped that someday, if the stars aligned, he might be able to prove that the abstraction of intangible thoughts were substantive realities – structures – that could be studied. They weren't memes. Someday…perhaps. He believed that. That would be a sea change for science and psychology, and even for a better understanding of human nature. It would question who we are: ourselves or a product of thoughts in the environment which infected us? Answering *that* question would cause quite an upheaval!

"It certainly would," said Ricardo, looking alert again. "That's exactly what I thought about jellyfish having a brain and seeing evolution. I imagined that would be a sea change in understanding animals. It didn't quite work out that way though. Too bad."

"Are you encouraging or discouraging me, Ricardo?"

"Yes, that's right."

"What's right?"

"I agree. Good luck, Roger. I can't wait to see what happens."

And then Ricardo, after being ambiguous, cryptic – *incoherent* – left Roger on his own again.

"Damn Ricardo," Roger muttered to himself, yet relieved to be rid of him for a while. He had a lot to think about.

158

Brainstorming

Roger woke up at night every few hours after his evening with Adam, worried whether he had underestimated the possibility that Thought-Particles were memes. He realized that memes didn't make abstract thought into a particle, but still, the idea that thoughts could be social genes, as Dawkins considered them, and travel through populations was ingenious. What did Robin think? She wasn't a scientist, but still, she had the intelligence that often outdid the complexity of scientific smarts. He felt it was time to evaluate whether he could come up with a case that was simple, insightful and believable if he wanted it to be publishable. What to do next? The one thing he knew he didn't want to do was collaborate with another scientist on this project. This was his baby, win or lose.

Robin had already gone out on an errand when Roger arose. He dressed, had a cup of coffee and a doughnut for breakfast and went to his study to jot down some ideas to outline a prospective article on Thought-Particles. A couple of hours passed without his realizing how quickly the time slid by when he heard Robin in the kitchen putting the groceries away. He needed a break and went to see her.

"Hi, Robin. Lots of good stuff to eat, I see. Any chocolate-hazelnut ice cream?"

"You bet. Want some?"

"It's tempting, but maybe for dessert tonight." Roger tried his best to control his appetite for sweets.

"Good for you. We'll pig out tonight! What are you up to now?"

Roger told her how he had slept fitfully, constantly thinking about memes. He said he was still worried that they might be a different name for Thought-Particles, which would undermine the novelty of his insight.

"I'm not so sure about anything anymore, Robin. What do you think?"

Roger put the food away while Robin made herself a cup of tea. She knew when Roger wanted to bounce his ideas off her, and she was always happy to play that role. In addition to helping him psychologically, she always learned something in the process. It turned out that she knew more science by listening to Roger organize his thoughts than most spouses of scientists who kept their work to themselves. How absurd! It was Robin's contention, and Roger's too, that science was only complicated when the scientists didn't understand it very well themselves.

They sat down at the kitchen table for a brainstorming session.

"Roger, if I understand correctly, you're thinking of a thought as some kind of packaged goods rather than simply a brain function. Correct?" she asked.

"That's about it."

"I love the idea, but it doesn't sound easy to prove or to get enough evidence to be convincing. Is that your problem – you feel that you don't have a strong enough case for Thought-Particles?"

Robin always tried to understand Roger's personal problem rather than the scientific one. But she was smart, loved science as a layman, and was an adherent of Occam's razor, namely the simplest of competing explanations for any phenomenon was usually the correct one.

"More evidence would be great," Roger said, "but I feel stuck. What I have already is really interesting, at least I think so, but…

"I accept that thoughts are in the brain, but I'm questioning how they got there, not what happens when they are in the brain. Neurobiologists believe that thoughts might be brain neurons firing in a particular circuit and changing functional connections, if I understand it correctly. But how would the circuits of firing neurons be transferred passively from one brain to another brain? In other words, how are the circuits set up and synchronized between brains? That neurons make specific and different functional corrections for each new idea seems difficult to explain. Anyway, thoughts don't all have to be created and processed in the same way. I'm suggesting that Thought-Particles are just one way for transferring thoughts with the receiver not even realizing how the new thought got there."

Robin thought quietly about that. "What about hypnosis?" she asked. "The brain somehow reaches a state that reacts to suggestions, but when the person wakes up, he or she can't remember anything. Isn't that a thought transfer – from a conscious brain to an unconscious one? Maybe Virerium puts the brain in a hypnotic-type state that absorbs suggestions. Would that work?"

"Good idea. Maybe. But that needs a person suggesting or directing the hypnotized person," Roger answered. "It's like brainwashing – mind control – a Big Brother of *1984* planting a thoughtcrime. Where is that authoritarian voice? I suppose it could have been Judy in Diane's case, or the Republican wife, and so forth. It would explain why the new thoughts were similar to those of the people closest to them. They're the so-called Big Brother, whether or not they intended to be."

"Have you got a better idea?" Robin asked.

"I've been doing some research about imaginative ideas – fiction, but still – of thoughts, dreams, the unconscious, and transfers from one mind to another. I know that you don't like science fiction or supernatural stuff, but sometimes the best ideas sound preposterous at first, like sci-fi, impossible, until someone shows that at least some of it is true. What about new music, which can sound like noise at first, but becomes popular when it has become familiar? That happened to Beethoven and Stravinsky in their day. They got terrible reviews, insults, until their music became known and accepted, and then they were idolized.

"Throughout history many ideas and inventions were considered fantasy, or never even imagined, before becoming reality. Think of flying or having rockets with cameras sending pictures of other planets back to Earth. Or maybe even the idea of toilets iin the dark ages! I'm still waiting to be beamed somewhere, as in the old TV series, *Star Trek*. I bet it will be possible eventually. Won't that be sensational! I'm all for it."

"So, what else do you have in mind?" Robin asked, almost as if she was ready to be inspired by science fiction for the first time.

Roger was on a talkative streak, bouncing ideas off Robin. Where would he have been without her?

Empowered by her attention, he brought up a classic novel that had stood the test of time – much time – *The Strange Case of Dr. Jekyll and Mr. Hyde*. In the story, one person splits into two personalities, back and forth. Written as a work of fiction, it turns out that such cases do exist in mental illness.

Truth? Fantasy? The question was when does fantasy become truth?

"That's different," countered Robin. "The Jekyll and Hyde personality switch is within one brain doing an internal transfer. It's brain regulation gone haywire, not one brain transferring a thought to another brain."

"Okay," Roger agreed. "But I remember watching *Inception*, the old movie from the early 21st century about implanting and transferring thoughts? A thief had a dream-sharing technology, called "inception," to steal secrets from the unconscious mind of a sleeping person and implant the thoughts into the mind of a different sleeping person. Isn't that foreshadowing what we're seeing in the Virerium pandemic, the acquisition and transfer of thoughts? What do you think?"

"I think it's time for lunch. I'm hungry. Let's eat."

Vale Wet, the Plumber

As they ate lunch, the conversation drifted from Roger's work to reminiscences of their Italian meal the day they first met. It was so simple then, so wonderful, when all they cared about was each other.

Suddenly Robin, looking down, exclaimed, "Hey, what's going on? There's a puddle on the floor! Where's the water coming from?"

"Oh my god, you're right! It's leaking from beneath the sink."

They opened the cabinet door under the sink, exposing the pipes, and there was the problem, more than a drip, yet not a full stream. Since Robin prided herself on not being able to fix anything, Roger tried being a plumber, as a dutiful husband might.

"Stop, Roger! You're making it worse. Look. You've started another leak above the original one."

"Oops. You're right." Roger turned off the main water pipe.

Robin called a plumber, called it an emergency, and a real plumber came in half an hour and fixed the, or rather, both leaks. The original leak was easily repaired by tightening a joint between two pipes. Roger's leak, on the other hand, was caused by his mangling a different joint so badly that it required a new pipe altogether. Roger dealt with the embarrassment by telling

Robin that from now on he would be careful to "pipe down." He also added, trying to save his ego, "It's not as bad as my mother, who started a fire in the kitchen trying to fix the oven."

Robin said she was proud of him for protecting her from the tsunami. "Not every woman is so lucky to marry a saint as a plumber," she said.

Nothing like a bit of diversion away from the difficulty of figuring out how to interpret Roger's data. But problems blend, like two small puddles of water approaching each other suddenly fusing to become one large puddle. Would Roger create a lake of problems by inept interpretation of his data?

All this hoopla about leaks and pipes was small potatoes compared to what the plumber – whose name, ironically, was Vale Wet – told Roger about his wife and money. As inevitable as small problems compound when they blend together, new insights often sprout from the least expected sources. The only rule which seems never to be violated is that life twists and curves in the most unpredictable fashion, making almost anything possible at any time.

"Thanks, Vale. You're a lifesaver. What a mess this would have been if you hadn't come to the rescue," said Roger.

"Yup, guess so," said Vale, without any expression on his face.

Roger glanced at Robin cleaning up the dishes from lunch and looking more involved in her efforts than Vale had been in his.

"Lucky I had the extra piece of pipe with the right dimensions in my truck," he said.

"I'll say. Makes me believe there is a God after all," Roger said facetiously.

Roger immediately caught his mistake, but it was too late. He had forgotten the cardinal rule to never mention politics, money or religion to anyone without knowing the background of that person. It usually ended badly for one reason or other. This time, however, it ended well.

"Maybe there's a God for you," said Vale in a monotone, "but God didn't help Gladys – she's my wife – or maybe God's punishing her for something. I don't know."

"Really?" said Roger, intrigued to learn more. He clearly had hit a responsive chord.

"Gladys goes to church every Sunday, that's more than I do," Vale said, wiping his hands on a piece of rag and starting to pack up his tools. "She always did, ever since she was a girl. Her stepfather was a minister, and she insists that we say grace before every meal."

"Sounds like a devoted Christian," Roger acknowledged, mildly uncomfortable with the turn the conversation was taking, but curious, nonetheless.

"Yup, sure is."

"So, how did God forsake her?"

"Forsake?'

"Abandon her."

"Well, one Sunday, when they passed the plate around for contributions," he began, plunging into an immediate digression. "They do that every Sunday. Frankly, it rubs me the wrong way, know what I mean? I work hard for my money, seven days a week, and taxes are bad enough. Gladys, she hasn't worked since the kids left, and that ticks me off. I wish she wouldn't give the church any more money every Sunday. I never told her that, because it's a touchy matter for her, but that's what I think."

That was the most excitement Vale had yet expressed. It was impossible to stop him now. His mood change was like a calm river narrowing into a stretch to become rapids. Roger waited to hear more, chastising himself a little for opening the conversation.

Vale complied.

"Anyway, that Sunday she said that she didn't have any change, and it turned out that she had said the same thing the Sunday before that. She felt bad about it, but you can't give what you ain't got. It's no big deal, as I see it. I'm glad that she didn't give anything. But then, damn it, her best friend, Valerie – kind of sounds like Vale, don't you think? – was sittin' next to her. They sit together in church every Sunday. Anyway, Valerie gave Gladys the evil eye, know what I mean?"

"You mean she was angry at Gladys for not putting any money on the tray?"

"Yup. That's it. Well, it made Gladys mad as hell, for her friend to turn against her like that, and she told Valerie to mind her own business. Valerie told her she was stingy and didn't appreciate how good the church has been to her, and so forth and so on. Gladys told her to shut up, and when Gladys says that she means it, and it's best not to mess with her. Anyway, she told her again to mind her own business. Valerie called Gladys a bitch, can you believe it? She called her best friend a bitch! Shit, she got a nerve. She went up to the preacher and told him that she gave extra this week because Gladys had given nothing for the last two weeks. Can you believe it? Shit."

"Valerie is the bitch, Vale," Roger agreed. "Why do you think she turned on Gladys like that?"

"I don't know, but I'm glad that Gladys didn't give any money away for a couple of weeks after that. I looked in her purse, I know I shouldn't do that, but I did, and what do you think I found? Money! She sure as hell did have some money, but she didn't want to give it away as she used to. When I asked her why, she said she changed her mind, that I worked hard for it, and it wasn't right for her to give it away. I'd been thinking exactly that and I was happy she finally understood. But here's the strange part. I started thinking that the church was her life after all, and maybe it wasn't that bad for her to support them a bit. I started thinking like she had thought, and she started thinking like I used to. Isn't that weird? And the switch happened at the same time. I'll say it is. Weird."

And then Vale stared into space, expressionless again. Maybe he was working the puzzle out, but it seemed more like he was the puzzle.

Roger didn't think it was weird. It was a Virerium-like switch, no different than a déjà vu phenomenon for him. This time it was a double switch: Gladys received her husband's thoughts, and Vale adopted hers. This had to be more than a coincidence.

"What do you think changed Gladys's mind?" asked Roger, not expecting an answer.

Vale started packing his equipment back in his box. Finally, after a long few seconds he said, "Beats me. All I know is that she caught a cold a couple of weeks before. Nothing serious, but she was feeling kind of lousy."

Gladys was sick! That was all Roger needed to hear. He thanked Vale for the help and tipped him a little extra. Even that didn't get much reaction from him, not like he had when he talked about Gladys and Valerie and the money issue.

The afternoon was eroding, Roger was tired, and Robin had gone out. Tomorrow was another day. Roger would mull over his ideas and attempt to draft an article in the morning to see if they held up under closer scrutiny.

He dreamt of a dam bursting and flooding their bedroom that night.

PART V

PUBLICATION

Roger's Article

Roger woke up at 6 a.m., an hour earlier than usual. It was still dark outside, and he was anxious to summarize the ideas that were swirling in his head. He dressed quietly in order not to wake Robin and tiptoed out of the bedroom. That wasn't entirely altruistic; he didn't want distractions, so it was best if she remained asleep. He had his morning coffee with cereal and went to his study, anxious, yet apprehensive, to start writing an article on Thought-Particles. It was one thing to be excited and proud of his insight as he developed the idea of Thought-Particles, when he (and Robin, of course) were the only critics. It was another thing altogether to publish Thought-Particles, to imply, "This is my best effort. It's who I am." Publishing gave every critic imaginable – students, peers, journalists – a chance to demolish the idea of Thought-Particles, to find fault, to ridicule the science and stab his heart. He imagined his head on a stake with a sign beneath that said to everyone, "Charlatan Scientist."

No, he thought. That's too dramatic. He could withstand those critics. He was a respected scientist. It didn't matter that he hadn't proved the existence of Thought-Particles yet; he was introducing the idea – a new insight – based on circumstantial evidence. He claimed nothing more. So, what was his concern? Whom did he fear?

His problem was the anointed group of elite scientists who resided smugly within the private circle from which he felt excluded, the Anthony Lunts, who glowed as they stood tall on the foundations built by the Sam Leemans of this world. Those were the ones from whom he felt excluded. It wasn't Thought-Particles at stake – it wasn't the science being judged – he felt that *he* was at stake – Roger Resin – his name, his contribution, his destiny.

As Roger battled his aspirations – feeling overwhelmed by his demons – Ricardo appeared, wearing his blazing orange socks.

"Roger, Roger, Roger. *Stop* all this nonsense. Stop now! Stop indulging yourself in your neurosis! Who do you think you are? Me? Are you afraid of being branded irresponsible and jailed, as I was? It's never just us, you know. Our fate is wrapped in the times we live. Do you think Galileo would be sentenced for heresy by the Church today? Of course not. Would I be vilified today for spending government funds on what was considered irrelevant research? No again. My era was an economic catastrophe in the midst of an outrageously conservative government. It's progressive times now. That's important. People are primed from the pandemic to appreciate the power of infection. Virerium comes to the rescue for you! Ha Ha! This is perfect timing for infectious Thought-Particles. So, go write the damn article."

"But what if Thought-Particles are nothing more than a figment of my imagination? Do you think I'll be fired, or laughed at?" Roger asked, hounded by the stigma of being wrong, or even ridiculous.

"Even Robin is worried," he added. "Why is that?"

"I have no idea what Robin's worried about. You have to ask her. But she's not you. Neither am I. Good grief. You have tenure at VSC, Roger. You're stuck, or I should say privileged, with who you are and where you are. And will you be laughed at? Only if you're funny, and that doesn't seem to be the case. I'm not laughing. If I were, I'd suggest that you write a funny novel instead of a science article. You're one of *them*, whoever you think they are. Prestigious circle of elite scientists? Give me a break. Anyway, don't count your chickens before they're hatched. Your article may not be accepted for publication. Then you would have the opposite problem. How to get it published?"

How good it was to have Ricardo by his side!

"I don't know, Ricardo. It's not about facts or reality. It's about belief, about honesty to oneself. It's who I believe I am, which seems truer than relying on who others think I am. Yes, belief, that's what it's all about. If I were Descartes I would say, 'I believe, therefore I am.' Don't you think that belief can be more powerful than facts sometimes? Isn't the history of science a list of discarded 'facts' replaced by new 'facts,' and so forth and so on?"

Ricardo frowned. "Belief, you say? Is that the truth? I believed, still do, that jellyfish have a brain and can visualize evolution. But…is it true?"

Ricardo disappeared as mysteriously as he had arrived. Here one minute, gone the next.

Roger went to his study, turned the computer on, and jotted down a few key words reminding himself to include different ideas in the article. His goal was a seamless narrative based on his observations and interviews building a case for Thought-Particles. He knew it would be difficult to convince his peers without proof that Thought-Particles existed. He needed the courage to plow on despite doubts that they might be products of his imagination, more science fiction than science.

Yet, at the same time, he *believed*, as he told Ricardo, even with a touch of arrogance, that Thought-Particles were real, perhaps revolutionary. Such conflict – doubt versus belief – was at the heart of discovery: doubt rumbled below the surface, while belief hovered above the clouds. Caught in this tug of war between illusion and reality, he prepared to enter the perilous journey.

"Fuck it, Roger," said Ricardo, who made another quick appearance to encourage him. "Start writing." Such foul language was unusual for the old-fashioned gentleman, so Roger took what he said seriously.

"It's your baby, Roger," continued Ricardo. "Thought-Particles are as real as you make them. Reality isn't just sitting pretty to be discovered. It can be as fickle as that which receives attention. Keep in mind that 'fact,' belief, whatever, can be justified in one era and not in another. You're in the right era for Thought-Particles, that's what I think, you lucky guy. I wasn't."

Roger set out to write a bold, unapologetic case for Thought-Particles, as Ricardo had encouraged him to do. He wanted Thought-Particles to stand on its own scientific merits. The most successful achievements – a discovery or technical advance – shed their creator and stood alone, as would a sturdy piece of useful furniture. On the other hand, he also wanted recognition as the discoverer of Thought-Particles. Who doesn't associate relativity or e=mc^2 with Albert Einstein, or the Mona Lisa painting with Leonardo da Vinci? He wanted to have Thought-Particles taught in every college and medical school biology class and featured in their textbooks. He wanted Thought-Particles to be his legacy. He wasn't modest in his thoughts.

Roger entitled his article simply "Thought-Particles." He proposed that Thought-Particles increased in frequency during the Virerium pandemic, which allowed him to deduce their existence. The heart of the article, the most innovative part, was the abstract concept of a thought transformed into a physical structure, albeit that structure still needed identification.

The article emphasized that Thought-Particles did not obviate other mechanisms for acquiring and transferring thoughts as well, hoping that coexistence of Thought-Particles with other mechanisms of having and transferring thoughts would prevent scientists from automatically rejecting the concept. He neither speculated on the composition of Thought-Particles nor dwelled on their implications, which he hoped to discuss in more detail in later publications. This article needed to give full attention to introducing the idea of Thought-Particles. With a modesty-be-damned attitude and influenced by the famous 1953 report on the structure of DNA by Watson and Crick, Roger concluded with the following sentence, which he placed in italics for emphasis.

"It has occurred to me that Thought-Particles suggest profound implications for free-will and social interactions."

He wrote the short article in one sitting. When he finished, he stretched his legs and breathed a sigh of satisfaction with a touch of apprehension. He looked around for Ricardo, who he expected to see at such a creative moment, but he wasn't there. Never mind. Roger went into the kitchen for another cup of coffee and found Robin having a late brunch, more like lunch than breakfast.

"You got up early," she said.

"I couldn't sleep and couldn't take my mind off Thought-Particles."

He helped himself to a slice of raisin toast, his favorite.

"Aren't you taking this too far?" she said, with uncharacteristic abruptness. "People get ideas, they talk, they trade stories and information. Who knows what happens when you're sick with a high fever, as the people you interviewed recovering from Virerium had been?"

Roger was taken aback by Robin's sudden cold, almost confrontational tone. What got into her? She seemed to believe in Thought-Particles the other day. What changed her mind? She always had helpful suggestions, even when his ideas went astray, and now she was questioning Thought-Particles and seemed upset. He felt a rising anger, a precursor to a fury that had erupted into outbursts in the past.

"Are you okay?" he asked brusquely.

"Yes, of course. I'm worried, that's all."

"About what?"

"About you making a fool of yourself. Do you really think that you can add anything to how people get thoughts, or how thoughts are transmitted? You're not a philosopher or a sociologist or psychologist. You're a biochemist or molecular biologist, or whatever it's called these days. You study genes and proteins. Because you study these in eyes doesn't mean you need to be a visionary scientist. Please, be careful. Things can be interesting without having them consume you. Is this something you actually want to publish?"

"Yes, it is," Roger said, in a quiet detached tone, feeling hurt. "Don't judge what you haven't even read."

He gave the draft to Robin for her opinion. After reading it she still worried that he had wandered from his scientific expertise and let his imagination run away. That was fine if discussing among colleagues or speculating in a lecture, but real science...a serious article in a scientific journal...a permanent, public exposure in a field in which he had no standing?

"No," she said. "I wouldn't publish it."

"Why are you so worried about my article or how Thought-Particles will be received? I don't get it, Robin. What's your concern?"

Robin blushed and fidgeted in her seat, suddenly looking insecure, somewhat lost, uncomfortable with herself.

"I'm not sure, Roger. Your research always was about gaining further knowledge of something tangible – a protein or gene or something that could be measured or seen. My opinion was useless, really, for all those things. I didn't know the science, and it was all facts, formulas, concepts. But Thought-Particles. They're so much imagination and unprovable. I don't know what to think. Will anyone?"

"So what? I'm just taking a chance on a wild idea. It's not fact...yet. I know that. It's still tenuous, an idea, a hypothesis at best at this point. Anyway, who knows if a journal will even publish it? At least, it can't be disproved any easier than it can be proved."

Robin shut her eyes, sighed and remained very quiet. Roger waited, giving her time and space to reflect, if that was what she was doing.

Eventually, he asked again, "What really bothers you?"

"It's God, Roger, or I should say religion. My parents were kosher, observant, devoted believers, as you know. They took me to services for years, I had a fancy Bat Mitzvah, but I never believed like they did, like they wanted me to believe. God? Religion? How could I reject such belief without any evidence one way or another? Belief strangled me. Belief is so ambiguous that there's no way to come to grips with it. You're lucky. An atheist has no problem. But an agnostic, like I was, probably still am, questioning belief and God, or something like that. But you keep asking for my opinion, like we're a team, like my parents always looked at me hoping that I believed like they did. They were family. We're family. It's just my vulnerability. Sorry."

Roger tried to understand. He had no patience for God or religion, and Robin looked tortured. Over what? Nothing, as far as he could understand. Her explanation seemed more for herself than about Thought-Particles.

More composed, she tried again.

"Imagine that you're under arrest for some crime," she said. "Wouldn't the lawyer tell you to volunteer as little as possible, to say nothing if you could get away with that, don't explain or excuse anything. Whatever you say could and would be used against you."

"I guess I'd keep quiet," he said.

"It's a jungle out there. Sharks eat little fish," she continued.

"Little fish?" He resented that implication. Maybe it was her tone of voice. Maybe it was his fear of being exactly that: a little fish.

Ricardo galloped into his mind, complaining that critics are idiots and should be ignored. "Speculation is the backbone of science. Forget the critics," Ricardo said. "Doesn't Robin realize that?" And then he went on a rampage. "How dare they put me in prison for wasting time and money for innovative basic research?"

Ricardo was still festering in anger from his fate so many years ago. Everything was mixing with everything else: Robin's conflict on religion, Ricardo's anger about his fate, Roger's uncertainty about Thought-Particles and frustration in his career. Little fish! Indeed! How confusing when the past contaminates the present, when the angst of others all blend, when nothing stands alone anymore. It's like being infected with Thought-Particles from every source, past and present, to influence the future.

Roger felt on the fence. He certainly didn't want to reenact Ricardo's fate. He couldn't do anything about Robin's conflict with religion. And he knew he wanted to publish his article. He wasn't about to abandon the project, nor was he doing it simply as a pastime.

After a moment, Roger finally asserted, "I *believe* in Thought-Particles, and if they don't exist, well, most new ideas are at least partially incorrect. But what if Thought-Particles are only partially correct? It's not about God or prison. It's an idea that I believe in. It's *my* idea. It's who I am, I guess."

He didn't really believe that Thought-Particles might not exist, but he wanted to be open-minded and objective. He was a scientist, not a charlatan.

Robin forced a smile.

How he loved her.

Roger went back to his study, looked over his list of ideas and observations and paced around the room. Ricardo was sitting in the comfortable armchair, which *was his* 100 years ago, smiling at him reassuringly, his orange socks in plain sight. This was not a social visit.

Roger surveyed his diverse books on the shelves, appreciating how many different interests he had, and at the same time belittling himself for how little he knew what was in those books. Shame on him for being too lazy to have read them all carefully and for having forgotten so much of what's in them. What was the point of reading if what he learned would be forgotten?

He rubbed his hand along an African staff as he passed by it and wondered what the tribal artist was thinking about when he carved this masterpiece. Was it as perfect as he hoped it would be, or were the figures he chose to sculpt too fanciful? There was no way of knowing what the artist thought or felt, and it didn't matter. What mattered now was what Roger thought of the staff.

Roger glanced at the Inuit sculpture of the kneeling caribou on his desk. Art and science reinforced each other, in Roger's opinion, in a brew made by humans for humans. Both were manmade, creative constructs.

And then there was Robin's religion conflict, and Ricardo's prison past, both of which congealed inseparably in his mind. There was no such thing as "present" time or "past" time. Time didn't move one way or another. It was always there, the same, no matter when. The cliché that time passes, or that the past was gone, or that the passage of time healed – what foolishness. Time stood still, so still that Roger thought sometimes that time didn't exist. All happenings, whenever they occurred, blurred together. He and Ricardo inhabited the same world.

Roger clasped his hands behind his back as he walked slowly back and forth in front of his desk. Then… then…with no warning…Roger had a surge of confidence.

Yes! Perhaps foolish or risky, certainly speculative, he would submit his article on Thought-Particles for publication. There was no artificial border that creativity shouldn't cross. Specu-lation – creative risks – was like everything else. It depended on a little knowledge mixed with optimism and a lot of belief. Every speculation had different degrees of validity. The exis-tence of Thought-Particles, his brainchild, was an entirely new concept, high risk, which also raised the possibility of huge rewards. The concept of Thought-Particles changed thoughts from an abstract concept to a substance – the essence of his insight and of his article – how many times did he need to repeat that to himself or anyone else? He hadn't seen the particle itself… true…and Thought-Particles hadn't been proved, far from it. Yet, have patience, he told himself. Don't rush creativity, which clarifies at its own pace. Science was historically specu-lative, sometimes fantasy preceded acceptance – robots and artificial intelligence and computers and voyages to the moon and beyond to outer space and exploration of ocean depths… and much more. The list went on and on and would continue to lengthen as people continued to think and create and take chances – all that fantasy which preceded acceptance was conceived in imagination, but also buried deeply in belief of some sort. Why exclude Thought-Particles?

Roger submitted his article to the prestigious journal *Science*. Possibly because he was a respected scientist, or possibly because of the novelty of the subject – thinking – or possibly due to the relevance of covering an aspect of the pandemic, Roger's article was accepted for publication.

And that initiated a chain reaction that changed Roger's life.

Anthony Lunt's Commentary

Roger's article didn't have any impact immediately after its publication. Five weeks later, however, *Science* published a brief comment from Dr. Anthony Lunt – *the* Tony Lunt, who had won the Golden Prize when Roger was a young member of the awards committee. Tony's comment was entitled ambiguously *SUBSTANTIVE THINKING: TRUE OR FALSE?* The first two sentences said it all:

"*Dr. Roger Resin, noted researcher at the Vision Science Center, suggests that thoughts are transmittable particles, literally a mysterious substance that infects our gullible brains. So much for intelligence or creativity or belief that we humans – Homo sapiens – can claim any superiority over dumb animals. Resin suggests that we are products of being randomly infected by particles, no better than robots being programmed by technicians.*"

"Don't say I didn't warn you," Robin said sympathetically over breakfast, doing her best to avoid any semblance of "I told you so."

"Yeah, I know."

"I'm sorry. It'll blow over, but…it's not terrible. After all, your imagination is one of the things I love about you, Roger. And you are courageous."

Ricardo whispered, "Courageous? A lot of good courage did me!"

Roger ignored him.

While some trivial comment or criticism could inflame Roger and trigger an outburst, this time it made him reflective. And as for Ricardo? "Big deal" to him too.

"I agree, Robin," Roger said. "My article didn't criticize or hurt anyone. It was an idea with supporting evidence. And you know what?"

"What?"

"Thought-Particles may be real, whatever Tony thinks. What a jerk he is! He's full of himself just because he got the Golden Prize award, which should have gone to what's his name – Sam Leeman. Maybe Tony has been infected with a Thought-Particle from a skeptic or a frustrated colleague who never had an original idea. Imagine, saying that Thought-Particles imply that animals are dumb, or that humans are like robots! How wrong, how wrong. Yes, wrong! I never said any of that. Where else did we get our smarts if not from animals? Doesn't Tony believe in evolution? There's tons of articles and books giving evidence that animals think. Ricardo published evidence a hundred years ago that thinking may have started already with jellyfish. Thinking and remembering. Someday his work will be appreciated. Not being appreciated or recognized is the curse of being ahead of the times."

"Thanks, Roger," said Ricardo. "I'm not sure I suggested that jellyfish actually think, but maybe they do. You're making me feel that hope springs eternal."

They finished breakfast in peace and then Roger went to the laboratory, as he did every morning, rain or shine, regardless of his mood.

When Roger entered the building, he felt self-conscious, as if everyone he passed in the hallways or who stood next to him in the elevator had read his article and then Tony Lunt's comments. Rather than pride for his innovative article, he felt embarrassed, even ashamed, as if Tony's negative remarks, no more than a needle in the haystack, had critically injured him.

Roger greeted his executive assistant, who responded with a cheerful, "Hello Roger!" when he entered his office. He preferred being on a first-name basis with everyone, secretary, students, anyone, regardless of position. Formality embarrassed him.

It was a normal day, no different than any other. He opened some mail left over from yesterday on his desk and looked out of the window when he heard a gust of wind outside. Dark clouds had taken over and started delivering heavy droplets of rain that were sliding down the window panes as tears.

He went into the laboratory to make sure his technician had started an experiment they had planned to do, and she had. What first caught his attention was the *Science* journal on her desk opened at the page of Tony's commentary. He felt like tossing it into the trash, but of course that wasn't an option, so he ignored it. No doubt the postdoctoral fellows had not only read it but had also discussed it. He imagined them saying, "Poor Roger," and that infuriated him. Best to ignore it, he thought, and he went about his daily routine, wondering what Ricardo thought about Lunt's response. Was he reluctant to say anything as well?

Roger was miserable all day.

At 4:17 in the afternoon, right after Roger had a cup of coffee by himself in his office with the door closed, the phone rang.

Nancy Weld, the Journalist

Roger let the phone ring multiple times since there had been a recent deluge of computer-generated fund-raising calls from every type of organization imaginable. Those calls invariably stopped after four or five rings. The phone kept ringing this time, so he answered.

"Hello."

"Is Dr. Resin there, please. Dr. Roger Resin."

"Speaking."

"I'm Nancy Weld, the science editor of the New York Times. Have you got a minute?"

The New York Times! Roger was put off balance. Was this true? The New York Times was interested in Thought-Particles? Had they read Tony Lunt's reaction?

"Oh, my goodness. Yes, I've admired your reports for a long time. They're excellent. Really."

"Thank you. Anyway, I read the opinion in *Science* by… Anthony Lunt, is that right? – about your report on Thought-Particles." Nancy was all business.

"Anthony Lunt. Correct?" she asked again. "It sounded to me like he didn't get the main point, so I looked up the original article. Thought-Particles seem intriguing, and definitely something new. Thought provoking. Newsworthy."

"Thought provoking? That's the right term. Thanks, I hope so. It seems that Tony Lunt didn't think so, but all he cares about is whether something is medically useful, not that that's bad. I've known him for years."

Roger's mind flashed back to the time that Tony received the Golden Prize award when Roger thought Sam Leeman deserved it. Was he destined to follow Sam's footsteps as a deserving loser?

Roger saw Ricardo standing in the back of the office. "Wow, Roger. This is exciting," Ricardo said. "The New York Times! Yeah!"

Ricardo was wearing his orange socks again, so he must have thought this was an important moment.

"How can I help you, Ms. Weld?"

"Please, call me Nancy. About your article. It's very different from other articles I've reported on, although I can't say I've read much, if anything, about where thoughts come from and how they might be transferred. It's strange to think about thinking! People talk and write and have abstract thoughts that dangle in the air for grabs. But you're saying thoughts can be actual particles, not just words or images. I want to hear more. I think that my readers may – should – want to hear more about this too. Are the particles the thoughts themselves, or do they convey the thoughts to the brain of the receiver?"

Roger listened to Nancy while Ricardo raised his eyebrows and mumbled, "Yeah, this is great, Roger. Be nice to her. She gets it."

Nancy continued, "Also, you gloss over possible implications of Thought-Particles in the last sentence of your article, which seems to me especially interesting. You teased us. Free will? Social interactions? What implications do you have in mind? Would you agree to an interview?"

Roger wasn't prepared for such an enthusiastic reception after swallowing Tony's bitter pill. Was Nancy Weld setting a trap of compliments only to write something even more damaging than Tony had?

"Yes, Roger," Ricardo said. "Of course, see her. But beware. She's a journalist, which means she's powerful. Tread with caution. But tread!"

Roger couldn't get The New York Times out of his mind. Nancy Weld was an unexpected gift. He'd published many articles on his research, solid scientific reports on various subjects within his expertise, yet none generated enough interest to invite him for an interview, much less by The New York Times. The irony was that scientists in his field were stingy to acknowledge his work, but now, when he dipped his toe into a field outside his area, in a field that Robin had warned him to not jump into, The New York Times came calling!

"When would you like to meet?" Roger asked, as matter-of-factly as he could.

"Tomorrow?" she proposed. "Is that too soon?"

"It's okay," he said, still pretending to be more accommodating than excited.

"Great. Should I come to your office?"

"Do you know where it is?"

"Of course," she said. "It's at the Vision Science Center. How about nine tomorrow morning?"

"I look forward to it."

"Until tomorrow morning."

Nancy arrived in his office precisely at 9 the next morning. She appeared in her mid-50s and was dressed conservatively – a study in gray – a gray skirt, gray blouse and gray shoes. The magnifying power of her horn-rimmed glasses, brown, not gray, emphasized her gray eyes. Oh, yes: she had gray hair.

Roger expected Ricardo to comment on all that gray, but he hadn't appeared yet. Maybe he wouldn't even come. He was dependably unreliable.

"Good morning, Dr. Resin. Thanks for meeting with me on such short notice."

Roger stood up behind his desk, smiled, shook Nancy's hand, and said, "It's my turn – Roger, please."

"Coffee?" Roger offered.

"Yes, thanks. Black, but lots of extra sugar."

"Sure," said Roger, in a friendly tone, not revealing his concern of what she might write about his work. The "extra sugar" worried him. Did she really like her coffee sweet, or was it a camouflage to "sugar coat" a bitter core? Roger didn't like being in someone else's control, especially someone else with power over him, like Nancy.

Ricardo did pop up after all. What a nuisance he could be, always able to read Roger's mind, yet…

"Stop being paranoid, Roger," Ricardo said. "Can't you just accept that this nice lady wants to understand more about Thought-Particles? You don't even need to have one of your outbursts to get her attention. Talk nice and she'll write nice. The only people who interviewed me about jellyfish were lawyers and prosecutors. They weren't nice!"

Roger relaxed, hoping Ricardo was right.

Roger and Nancy sat by the table that he used for spreading data, forms, manuscripts – any documents. She stirred her sweetened coffee, while he sipped his, black without cream or sugar. He was self-conscious about his weight and tried to keep his cholesterol levels in check. Roger always needed something to obsess about, poor guy. And he didn't want to be pudgy, as Ricardo was.

"Roger, I've read your article on Thought-Particles, but would you mind just summarizing it to make sure I haven't misunderstood anything?"

That's a good start, he thought, as his tension released. When he focused on the work –Thought-Particles – he forgot about career and reputation – about himself – and became engrossed in the larger world of science and ideas. For all his neurotic notions, Roger was passionate, honest as the day is long, and in love with science.

He told Nancy about Thought-Particles and briefly summarized his reasoning.

"I stress proximity, Nancy," he said. "I know it sounds obvious that things next to each other are in the best position to influence one another, or to transfer Thought-Particles, whatever they might be. Remember, the thought transfers I'm talking about happened in the absence of dialogue or anything written. Diane adopted the personality of her close friend Judy. The same occurred for the other acquisition of new thoughts I told you about. Theoretically, I presume, Thought-Particles could be transferred over larger distances, depending on their stability and other properties, but we don't know anything about that."

Roger was careful not to speculate too much or say anything he would regret later.

"What about memes, Roger? Dawkins made a big deal about that years ago. He cleverly called memes a social counterpart of genes. Could your Thought-Particles be another name for memes?"

Roger stiffened. He hadn't mentioned memes in his article since he had discarded them as possibilities in his discussion with Adam. But Nancy had done her homework and needed a response. Was her "sugar-coated veneer" eroding? Roger thought her tone of voice reflected more her point of view than a question. He had to be cautious. To beware.

Roger glanced around the room looking for Ricardo, but he was nowhere in sight.

He told Nancy he had considered that Thought-Particles might be memes, but there were stark differences between the two. He painstakingly summarized the arguments against memes being Thought-Particles, as he had hashed out with Adam, stressing that a meme is an abstract entity that spreads throughout the population, like a fad and becomes part of a common culture.

"Thought-Particles aren't like that. They aren't memes, Nancy. Memes can be ideas, tunes, catch-phrases, skills, pictures – many things. It's true that they are conceptually a type of 'unit' that infects brains, and spread by imitation, repetition and word-of-mouth. according to Dawkins. They might be considered analogous to a virus in their ability to spread, but not like a Thought-Particle. For a meme to survive, it has to invade the culture. Dawkins considered memes social genes and propagated for their own advantage, as a form of natural selection, except it was cultural selection – units of cultural evolution, as it were – while genes, DNA, were units of physical evolution.

"Well," Nancy said, sounding authoritative, "isn't that somewhat your view of Thought-Particles?"

Roger's inner volcano began to smolder and threatened to destroy his composure. Wasn't she listening? Didn't she understand anything? Thought-Particles weren't memes. His previous outbursts in Dr. Thomas's office and at the study section flickered in his mind, like kindling initiating, no, inciting, the flame. How dare Nancy Weld – a journalist, a science layman at best, a person who spent her life writing about other people's creativity, who probably had never come up with an original concept herself – have the gall to challenge his interpretations?

Roger's ire was gaining strength when Ricardo's image entered his mind, this time sitting in the witness box at his trial being interrogated by the prosecutor for the crime of irrelevant research and fiscal irresponsibility, and suggesting he was a fraudulent scientist.

Wait! Ricardo was being interrogated in a trial, and he was fighting for his life to keep out of jail, while Roger was being thoughtfully questioned about Thought-Particles by a curious journalist. Ricardo lost his battle; Roger planned to win his, or at least do everything possible to do so. Suddenly becalmed, as a sailboat in the absence of wind, Roger stalled.

"Memes are interesting, Nancy," he said, using his professional voice. "They are an interesting concept, but in my opinion, they aren't Thought-Particles."

"Exactly how are they different?" Nancy asked, her tone softening, sounding less judgmental.

"Don't be lazy, Roger," said Ricardo, now leaning against the back wall. "Nancy needs to understand the difference between memes and Thought-Particles, or she might write that Thought-Particles are just re-invented memes. You can't allow that to happen."

Roger nodded at Ricardo and said in silence, with his lips alone, "Thanks. You're right."

Ricardo mimed back for Roger to lip-read, "You're welcome."

"Several reasons," Roger told Nancy. "Thought-Particles are more targeted than memes and more limited. They infect brains but they don't spread widely as memes. They are transmitted like thoughts between two people close to one another. Thought-Particles float in the air and physically enter the brains of the recipients. Thought-Particles are just that – particles. Memes are concepts."

"But, Roger, you didn't look past the people you interviewed. How do you know how far Thought-Particles spread?"

Was she provoking him to extract more information, or was she was looking for a quote she might use? She sounded like Adam. Did she know him, perhaps? Adam knew a lot of people.

"Good point, Nancy," Roger countered, keeping his composure. "Look, here's the pivotal point. Thought-Particles act in the immediate environment. I think that proximity is key. A Thought-Particle can introduce a thought to someone without that person ever realizing it. I guess that a person could express a thought in many ways – speaking, writing – including Thought-Particles that infect other people. If the thought in a Thought-Particle goes viral, I suppose it could *become* a meme, but that meme would not be the particle itself; it would be the result of the particle. I don't think, although I admit that I don't know for sure, that the particle itself could go viral. For every transmission, it must be released by someone, although I admit, we don't know how that happens, and then it must be received by someone close by, which we also don't know how that happens.

"The original Thought-Particle ain't no meme!" Roger said emphatically, trying to hide behind slang to sound friendly.

Nancy didn't react to "ain't," nodded and then removed her glasses, as some people do to display how wise they are. That always seemed pretentious to Roger.

Roger added that Thought-Particles didn't seem to have anything to do with cultural evolution, an important role Dawkins attributed to memes. He stressed, once again, that Thought-Particles were simply thoughts packaged as a substance being physically transferred between two people.

"Okay. I get it," Nancy said, finally.

"Look, all science is a mix of facts accepted as truth at the time, riddled with assumptions, which is another way of saying conjecture," Roger said, sounding more confident and somewhat professorial, "but I haven't mentioned what I think is potentially the most important aspect of Thought-Particles."

Nancy perked up. "I'm all ears. Go for it."

"By its very name, a Thought-Particle is a substance, an infectious particle which has some kind of structure, like a virus. But it isn't a virus, in my view. Thought-Particles don't create pandemics, like viruses do. They carry thoughts. Period. Since a Thought-Particle has never been seen, it's still speculative, but that doesn't mean that they don't exist."

Roger added, somewhat redundantly, "Here's the important point. Thought-Particles make an abstract thought into something particulate. Once a Thought-Particle has been isolated, which I'm betting will happen someday, hopefully while I'm still alive, I believe it will create a new path into the human brain, and maybe also into animal brains. Thought-Particles could be a game-changer for understanding the generation of ideas or of thinking itself. Oh, my god, Nancy, I believe Thought-Particles have so many implications, I don't know where to start."

Nancy checked her watch and, surprised, said, "It's already 11:30, Roger. I had no idea where the time went, and I have another appointment at noon, which will not be as interesting as speaking with you. Could we continue tomorrow, or if not, another day?"

"Sure, but I've really said everything I know. I don't think I can add much."

"Spoken like a scientist who is just getting started," she said, with a wink. "I'd love to dive into your last sentence in the article about the implications of Thought-Particles. That's the real meat at this point, wouldn't you say?"

They adjourned until 9 the next day, and Roger went for an early lunch. Had he been clear in speaking to Nancy? Had he said too much or not enough? He loved to torture himself!

Now he had to decide what implications he would tell Nancy tomorrow morning.

Implications

That night, Roger made a list of possible implications of Thought-Particles, but he knew he was stretching credibility in some cases. He may have had an imaginative story, but it had weak legs. Yet, he believed the implications were reasonable, as much as Ricardo believed that jellyfish had brains and visualized evolution. Ricardo had his evidence; Roger had his. Neither had proved anything.

But Nancy would be there in the morning, and he needed to follow up with implications. He had to have a convincing story to tell her. Wasn't that the plight of being human – being challenged by each step forward? Wasn't dealing with situations the plight of being alive? That could mean gloating with a moment of success or confronting obstacles that suddenly appear. Implications of Thought-Particles were a bit of both. The present is never static. It's always new, every minute is novel; being alive is accepting and dealing with that reality. Roger had to deal with what he had created. He was alive. Assuming Thought-Particles were true, what were their implications?

"Good morning again, Roger," said Nancy. She arrived exactly on time.

"Same to you."

"You were going to tell me your ideas about implications of Thought-Particles."

Roger fidgeted in his seat. Nancy removed her notebook from her briefcase, preparing to take notes.

"I'm not sure where to start," Roger said.

"How about the beginning?"

He smiled. "Okay. Let's go back to the 17th century in France and René Descartes. Mind you, I'm not a philosopher. These are just some ideas I've had."

Nancy nodded. "I know. Just pretend I'm not here."

"That's a tall order, Nancy," Roger said, realizing that his greatest fear was not exploring his thoughts, but exposing them to ridicule. He had often said that exposure was necessary to test credibility. There were many times he had felt strongly about one thing or another, but when he spoke about it, he wasn't so sure anymore. It was like reading poetry: it had one meaning when read silently and another when read aloud. Fear of the opinion of others always challenged him to a higher, more critical level. He felt that challenge now; he was not so sure of himself and worried about saying things he didn't understand in enough depth or, perhaps, didn't even mean.

"What's true or false, or reality or illusion, has been extensively debated. Do you agree, Nancy? Descartes wondered if our sense of the world could be an illusion. I gather his famous, 'I think, therefore I am,' meant that that we fabricate our reality, at least that's how I understand the comment."

Roger paused for a moment and looked at Nancy for reassurance to go on. He wasn't an authority on Descartes or any other philosopher; he was simply relating his ideas.

Nancy didn't budge or say anything, so Roger continued.

"I'd say that Descartes' 'I think' implied then, and still does today, that we generate our thoughts about reality through our senses, making our 'reality' an illusion. However, if we can receive Thought-Particles passively – if thoughts are physical structures that infect us at random – the question adds the ambiguity of 'what do we believe is reality' to 'who are we?' Are we ourselves or are we a combination of the people whose thoughts were transferred passively to us via Thought-Particles? And to make it even more complicated, the thought-donors received their thoughts passively from others? 'We,' the recipients of Thought-Particles, lose a lot of credibility as autonomous individuals. Each of us becomes a node in the large network. 'We' are really a synthesis of numerous other people – we are 'they,' bits of multiple other people. What do you think about that?"

"Interesting, but isn't that also true even if Thought-Particles don't exist? We are constantly influenced by others. We live in a society. Face it, we are herd animals. How do Thought-Particles change that?"

"They change that by not giving us a choice. Thought-Particles infect us randomly, depending on who is nearby and what Thought-Particles they release. We have a choice of whether or not to believe what we hear or read, but we don't have that choice if we're infected with a Thought-Particle by chance. Diane didn't choose to change her personality. Donors don't have a choice on what Thought-Particle they release, and recipients don't have a choice of what Thought-Particle infects them. It's a random biological process. It's like catching Virerium, or any virus in the vicinity, which isn't targeted to infect a particular person. The recipient neither chooses to be infected with a Thought-Particle nor is even aware of being infected. The Thought-Particle – which becomes the thought – is acquired silently and passively; it's chance, not choice. We may not be as smart or independent thinkers as we would like to be."

Roger paused a moment before exclaiming, "Oh, Nancy, this is huge! You and I are echo chambers of Thought-Particles we've received from the environment!"

Roger had crossed the barrier of self-consciousness. He was skidding down a self-generated slope. He spoke his mind. It was an outburst in reverse, a positive passion, as uncontrolled as his outbursts of anger. Out of control anger and unrestricted jubilation – the capacity for one complemented the capacity for the other. Would he be rewarded for that as he was for his angry outbursts?

"You mentioned free will in your article, Roger?" Nancy asked. "Do you mean that Thought-Particles take away freedom to have our own thoughts if our thoughts drift in from the environment?"

"You're on the right track, Nancy. Free will has been a mind bender throughout history. I've done a bit of reading about that. The mathematician Pierre-Simon Laplace in the 19th century seems to be a major voice about free will, or I should say the absence of free will, which he considers an illusion. However, he didn't propose Thought-Particles. He created a demon of sorts – the Laplace demon – which contains all the information possible in the world – the forces, particles, velocities – everything that exists in the universe, and he claims that demon governs our thoughts and actions, not free will. I believe that Thought-Particles add randomness to the deterministic Laplace demon, unless Laplace would say that even random motions are determined. I guess he would, but I don't. I believe that Brownian motion – random movements of tiny particles – is not directed; it's molecules being bombarded by other molecules."

"How's Brownian motion relevant to Thought-Particles, or did I miss something?" Nancy was trying her best to understand

Roger, who was flooding her with too many ideas for her taste, and probably too much philosophy for him!

"You didn't miss anything, Nancy. I know I'm rambling. It's a bad habit of mine. But you asked for implications, which are always cooked-up ideas, somewhere between possibility and nonsense. How is Brownian motion connected with Thought-Particles? Good question. Why did I bring that up?

"I guess random bombardments of atoms and molecules on a Thought-Particle, which would give it the energy to move about, could drive it towards a nearby brain by chance. It would be a low probability, but possibly a high impact, event. However, we have no idea how many Thought-Particles are floating around, or how much energy or how long it takes for a brain infection. That's science for you, lots of unknowns. The details of how Thought-Particles get extruded or engulfed into a brain are fields within themselves, and I have nothing to offer about those."

Roger was suddenly struck with a new thought. Speaking always gave him new ways to look at things. Virerium patients had high fevers, which generated heat. Could that energy from fever heat drive Thought-Particles out of or into brains more rapidly than usual, or cause Brownian motion to accelerate, speeding up their movement from one brain to another, or give them added energy to get into brains? Anyway, all that was too iffy to talk about. Nancy could take only so much.

But she was resilient. She stopped writing and asked Roger whether, in his opinion, all thoughts were ultimately from Thought-Particles.

"No, absolutely not," Roger said "I made that clear in my article. Nature is encompassing and robust. Nothing is all or none or only one way. I believe that Thought-Particles are just one source of thoughts. I don't eliminate internally generated thoughts, books, conversations, and other mechanisms for having thoughts. Thought-Particles don't displace other mechanisms of having thoughts. They're something in addition to consider, a new possibility. I have no idea what proportion of anyone's thoughts might come from Thought-Particles or from other sources. That will depend on the person and their environment. But I do think that Thought-Particles have implications relevant to societies or culture in general."

"Like what?"

"Let's see, how about...anarchy?"

"What? Anarchy?"

"Maybe that's stretching credibility," said Roger. "But consider this: many of the random Thought-Particles will be contradictory. The thought itself depends on whose brain emits it, and how it's interpreted depends on the closest brain that receives it. It's always a matter of chance. The content of the Thought-Particle, as well as the receiver, are unpredictable. If Thought-Particles are more common than we imagine, and there could be lots of them, each emitted by chance and randomly accepted, they would distribute a bundle of different views and opinions and thoughts, helter-skelter, without any central control or message, no 'Big Brother' of any type. Thought-Particles are not for propaganda or brainwashing. They're a melting pot of chaos. That's what I'm calling anarchy – *thought* anarchy. Yes, *a melting pot of chaos*. I like that."

Nancy didn't look convinced. "It sounds more like democracy to me. Everything is on the table."

"Maybe," said Roger, "but it's the random nature of Thought-Particles that I think have the most implications."

Suddenly, there was Ricardo again, grinning from ear to ear. "You're getting pretty heavy handed, Roger. Be careful that no one commits you for insanity. That would be quite an end, no? I went to jail for irrelevant research, and you go to the nuthouse for insane thoughts. Two peas in a different pod!"

Roger suddenly thought of himself as an example of a random collection of diverse thoughts. He imagined that he received Thought-Particles from his mother, Beatrice, an actor emitting all kinds of thoughts from plays and eclectic crowds in New York, certainly a beehive of diverse Thought-Particles. The thought contagion must be enormous in such environments.

After a short pause, Nancy said, "Thanks so much, Roger, for sharing your insights. I need to mull all this over."

"Will I get a chance to see a draft of your article before it's published?"

"No. It's forbidden. That would be counterproductive to an objective review. We must maintain what we are meant to be – a free press."

"But what if you misrepresent what I've said? It's been a bit of a mishmash."

Nancy hesitated, searching for the right answer. "Well," she said, "all news is partly true and partly wrong, but not necessarily fake on purpose. To some extent, news is similar to Thought-Particles. What's selected is a bit random and can have unpredictable effects. Is that anarchy or democracy?"

"Both, I guess," were Roger's parting words.

Ricardo reappeared, expressionless, looking lonely and older than usual. He had nothing to say for a change. Roger wasn't sure whether that was good or bad.

Nancy's Article

Roger checked the New York Times every day, looking for Nancy's article. Finally, after a month, he was happy to see it in the Op-Ed section. He had expected her article to be in the Science section, but the Op-Ed section gave him much wider exposure. The article read smoothly and stated accurately what he had told Nancy. The large lettering of the headline, "THOUGHTS AS PARTICLES" made it jump out of the page. Also, his name was mentioned in the first sentence, another benefit: *"Roger Resin, a scientist at the Vision Science Center, has proposed a startling new theory, namely that our thoughts can be delivered by particles emitted from people in close proximity..."*

She reported accurately how his observations of acquired thoughts and opinions, and even personality changes, by recovering patients from Virerium illness led to his proposing Thought-Particles. Instead of claiming implications of Thought-Particles, should they exist, Nancy wrote about questions they raised. Are we autonomous individuals or simply a tiny part of a colonial organism, a node in a giant network? Do Thought-Particles challenge free will? How would they affect demographics? She mentioned briefly the anarchy versus democracy question. Nothing in the article was blatantly incorrect. Roger's one disappointment was its overall presentation, which lacked the sense of excitement he felt. It sounded like an interesting report, rather than a novel insight.

"What do you think, Robin? Is it a good article?"

"Absolutely," she answered without hesitation. "I'm relieved. Nancy understood what you said, expressed it clearly, and gave you credit. You dodged the potential bullet. Congratulations. Now you can go back to work on your regular research."

"I guess you're right...it's accurate...but...I don't know... it's flat."

Roger was hard to please. No, make that impossible to please.

"The questions that Nancy proposed are what we talked about," he said, "but she didn't catch the novelty of Thought-Particles. By themselves, facts and questions don't pack a wallop. They need to be...what?...be humanized...incorporated into a paradigm shifting narrative to have an impact. The world is jolted by insights and discoveries when they change the way we think and make the impossible possible and change fantasy to reality. I believe Thought-Particles are in that category – brand new, surprising, overflowing with implications – change the way we think – and need to be portrayed that way. The messenger can be as important as the message for maximum impact. She didn't achieve that. She's smart, but not that messenger."

Roger took a moment to catch his breath. Ricardo grasped the interval to make his entrance.

"You're in the zone, Roger," he said. "That's just the way I felt about the apathetic response when I suggested jellyfish had brains and visualized evolution. What a lack of imagination! At least no one is criticizing you like they did me. Be grateful for little favors."

Roger wasn't in the mood to listen to Ricardo, and he silently begged him to go away, which, remarkably, he did. That was unusual!

Energized, Roger continued his monologue.

"Who cares about antibiotics if no one died from an infection, or what difference would the structure of DNA make if it wasn't the template for heredity and life itself? A collection of facts doesn't get attention; it's the compelling narratives they create, how our lives are changed by them, or how they change insecurity to confidence, or sometimes unfortunately, vice-versa. It's not the questions, it's the unexpected answers that excite and clarify confusion.

"Understanding the total eclipse of the sun removed the mystery of sudden midday darkness, which cavemen must have taken as the wrath of God. It's the *significance* that counts," he almost shouted. "Nancy considers Thought-Particles like…well, *interesting*. That's about as weak as saying that someone is *nice*. 'Nice' is boring. So is 'interesting.' What do those terms mean? They're too relative or soft to have impact. At least consider how nice differs from not nice, or how interesting differs from not interesting."

"Is that all, Roger?" Robin asked. "Let me know when you're done."

"As a matter of fact, there's more," he said, reacting to her sarcasm.

Roger wondered why Robin couldn't see how shallow Nancy's article was, how she failed to show the originality and importance of Thought-Particles, which started a new way to think about thoughts and even human nature. Nancy never stressed that Thought-Particles gave substance to the abstraction of thinking. She barely suggested it.

Although Ricardo had left the scene, he remained in Roger's mind. He considered Thought-Particles comparable to Ricardo's insight elevating jellyfish from a 'glob' to a creature with a brain, and how he and Ricardo had both provided steppingstones in the evolution of thinking and consciousness. Maybe he should go to La Parguera in Puerto Rico, as Ricardo had done, and look for Thought-Particles in jellyfish, where they might be easier to visualize.

Exhausted by his own stream of consciousness, Roger paused. He knew he was going astray, rambling, but he was who he was, as we all are, ourselves, filled with Thought-Particles from multiple sources interacting with our genes, which have been derived from our predecessors and mutated over accumulated generations, making it far too complex to understand or predict.

He had one last surge of complaints, a parting, self-serving song.

"Nancy should have presented Thought-Particles as an important scientific insight with eye-popping implications, both positive and negative, that needed, no, *demanded* further research," Roger said. "Oh, what do I know? I should have gone more deeply into implications with her. You're right, Robin, at least the article seems…harmless."

Robin looked relieved that Roger had finally finished his rampage.

"Don't underestimate harmless," said Ricardo, who materialized again for a breath of air.

"That's what I did, Roger…not take implications seriously enough…considered *relevance* irrelevant…*harmless*…well, you know the result."

And then, poof, gone again. Gone with the wind.

What Roger meant by "harmless" was that he wouldn't be indicted as Ricardo had been after he published his jellyfish article. There wouldn't be a trial connected with Thought-Particles, not in Roger's more liberal era. He wouldn't be indicted or go to jail for innovative research.

But there's always the other side of the coin, thought Roger, more constructively. Maybe "harmless" means something positive, the opposite of harmful, not neutral, but something that could enhance his legacy. After all, he was the first to think of transforming the abstraction of a thought into a substance. Maybe his legacy would enter the ranks of a visionary, despite Robin's warning about not trying to be a visionary. Perhaps both Ricardo and Roger would become visionaries. Wouldn't that be something! Ricardo Sztein and Roger Resin, who shared a genetic heritage five generations apart, both noted as prophetic scientists, visionaries.

It depended on the unpredictable future. And truth, of course. Truth.

Speculations

Although Roger worried that Nancy had short-changed the significance of Thought-Particles, her article wasn't ignored. Scientists gave their viewpoints in subsequent publications. Rather than being pleased to have his concept newsworthy, Roger's skill in finding flaws continued to haunt him, and he was disappointed that no scientist seemed to consider Thought-Particles as seriously as he had hoped.

Most physicists – but not all – said it was impossible to investigate Thought-Particles further. A few, however, had fun playing with ideas. They compared thoughts with gravity, a force comprising gravitons, and with light, a stream of illumination comprising photons. Neither had mass but could be described as quanta in an electromagnetic field, and the quanta idea resulted in a wave-particle duality. And that brought in the famous uncertainty principle, namely, that electrons could be described as waves or particles, but not both at the same time. What if Thought-Particles were both waves and particles depending on how they were viewed? Perhaps a Thought-Particle was an elementary particle – a "thoughton" – which escaped as a wave from the donor's mind and became a particle in the receiver's mind.

Despite all this discussion, the Thought-Particle idea didn't catch on. It was too vague and ambiguous and lacking in concrete evidence. It was essentially untestable. Nonetheless, a few physicists continued to wonder "thoughtons," wave/particle duality...possibly... interesting...maybe...maybe not...

Astronomers made the analogy, reluctantly, that Thought-Particles might be the biological equivalent of dark matter, which was also predicted strictly by observation and circumstantial evidence, but its identity remained unknown. One astrophysicist wondered if Thought-Particles might be related to the cold dim residual light of the universe – the faint glow that couldn't be accounted for by the light coming from stars – another physical phenomenon that was noted but not understood.

Biologists were more down to earth (literally). They considered Thought-Particles as submicroscopic specks of a mysterious substance with an attached thought, but they had no idea what substance might comprise the thought. Biologists bantered back and forth whether a Thought-Particle might have a complex structure, like a virus, or whether it might be a simple scaffolding with a thought latched to it and released in the brain of its new host. As for its chemical composition, perhaps a lipid with attached water-soluble compound would do the trick. The combination might give them a fighting chance to get through both hydrophobic and hydrophilic layers on its journey from brain to brain.

Biologists considered the possibility of a Thought-Particle code. One scientist suggested a conformational thought code rather than a chemical code like DNA, although a combination of both might be the case. Various thoughts could be represented by different shapes of the same substance. Even tiny differences in angles or other conformational variations could represent different thoughts. Reference was made to Stanley Prusiner, a Nobel laureate more than 100 years earlier, who showed that a conformational change in a protein (called a prion) transmitted information to other proteins, leading to a neurodegenerative disease. Why exclude Thought-Particles from the power of conformation?

Some biochemists imagined that a Thought-Particle might be a messenger activating a latent thought already in the receiver's brain. Many hormones worked as messengers that activated various biochemical responses. "Okay," some biochemists said, "but that just kicks the problem downstream, making a Thought-Particle a Thought-Hormone, and that leads to the enigma of what the particle is and what reactions it triggers."

Other speculations by biochemists had some similarity to those by physicists. One suggested that a Thought-Particle might be an electromagnetic wave or sonar, like bats have. Another idea was that near infrared light, which could penetrate the skull and brain tissue, might play a role in Thought-Particles. The most far-out suggestion was that Thought-Particles could be a bundle of neutrinos that could go through a human skull like a hot knife through warm butter.

Every speculation was fair game. Ideas were cheap – just mere words. No scientist was sufficiently convinced to explore the possible existence of Thought-Particles, which oscillated between conjecture and science fiction – pure fantasy.

Roger was increasingly depressed with all these haphazard notions, which he considered more appropriate for a movie or a surreal sci-fi novel than science. He vented his frustration to Robin, bemoaning, "What can be expected when imaginative research takes a back seat to nonsense," although he had to admit that some of these ideas were interesting.

Ricardo liked the Thought-Particle concept in general and kept an open mind as to whether Thought-Particles really existed. He was convinced that the ability to think had started early in evolution and Thought-Particles might provide a handle to study thought evolution. However, he was sad to see Roger disappointed. Once, when Roger was in the doldrums after reading a negative review of his article, Ricardo appeared to cheer him up. Being a soft-hearted, inspirational friend, Ricardo came adorned in glistening steel armor and riding a white horse.

"Forget it, dear Roger," said the gallant Don Ricardo. "These scientists may be fools, but hey, they're talking about Thought-Particles. They sense something interesting, maybe even more interesting than you realize. They're just jealous and, I'd say, a little scared of you."

"Scared? You've got to be kidding."

"Scientists are competitive, as you and I both know, and I'm sure they're impressed with Thought-Particles, at least with your notion of Thought-Particles. Dulcinea, oh how sweet she is, taught me to have faith and a little patience. She said it will all work out in the end if you stick to your dreams."

Roger didn't have much faith in Dulcinea and was losing confidence in his dreams, yet he was buoyed by Ricardo's optimism. He was impressed, as always, how the spirit can exceed reason and how truth hides until it finds an appreciative home.

What neither Roger nor Ricardo, nor Robin, nor anyone else for the matter, could have predicted was that a little patience and a bundle of optimism would pay off, but in a fashion that no prophet could have imagined.

Sociologists and Psychologists

Unexpectedly, a few weeks later sociologists joined the feeding frenzy on Thought-Particles. A glimmer of hope for the fate of Thought-Particles peeped through the cracks. Maybe Ricardo – or rather Dulcinea – was right. He needed patience and a firm clasp on his dreams. Thought-Particles began to wander outside the realm of hard science.

The social scientists harped on the idea that Roger had expressed to Nancy: he called it anarchy, while she called it democracy. The notion was that Thought-Particles might bind people together by being infected with the same thoughts, while also maintaining diversity by a flux of differing thoughts constantly jumping around randomly among those in the environment. The sociologists compared the effect of Thought-Particles on societies with how multiple species of trees thrive when linked by symbiotic associations of fungi and roots in connections called mycorrhizas. That's how forests flourished – by sharing nutrients and whatever else they needed when they needed it. Individual trees in spacious conditions weren't as healthy. Perhaps tribes and villages and cities thrived by having Thought-Particles as symbiotic agents creating networks with multiple nodes of similar and differing thoughts – a silent network of interacting thoughts passively transferred every which way – an invisible structure of coherence.

"Hey Roger, Thought-Particles seem to have broken the barrier of hard science! The sociologists took the bait," said Ricardo, who rushed to celebrate when he heard that Thought-Particles had been noted by sociologists.

"Yeah. That's great," said Roger. "It's just what Nancy and I discussed. Remember? They must have been eavesdropping. I called this the anarchy of thoughts, while Nancy preferred to think of it as democracy. Maybe she's right – everything is on the table all the time, with similar and different thoughts in one big puddle of chaos."

After this boost by sociologists, psychologists leaped into the discussions and targeted free will. Half of the articles said that Thought-Particles might be a plug for determinism – the eradication of free will due to programming people into robots. They warned that Thought-Particles could be used for brainwashing, propaganda or advertisement, or even to induce hallucinations, making people "see" what's not there. More positively, on the other hand (everyone has two hands), Thought-Particles might help people to overcome bad habits, or even to rehabilitate criminals. All of this would occur passively, without notice, by infection with Thought-Particles. So much for free will, said those psychologists. Thought-Particles ruled and determined outcome.

The other half of the psychologists proposed that Thought-Particles could have an opposite effect and be used to demonstrate free will by testing for the ability to overcome being programmed. Neuropsychologists even wondered whether Thought-Particles might be identified by probing brain regions known by electrical and metabolic activity studies to be the sites of cognition and thinking.

Roger was happy to see Thought-Particles receiving so much attention, but still he believed that such speculations were worthless, although perhaps useful to keep in mind.

Ricardo agreed.

"What do you think about all these articles by sociologists and psychologists?" Roger asked Robin one night during a candle-light dinner in the small Italian restaurant where they shared a spaghetti dinner the day they first met.

"Pretty exciting," she said, "although there's so much not known yet. It's all like skating on thin ice. I'm not sure Thought-Particles, if they exist, will ever be identified in our lifetime. Don't hold your breath."

"I won't," he said, happy at least that now she seemed not to discard the notion of Thought-Particles altogether, although he realized she wanted to support him, whatever the scientific truth turned out to be.

They agreed that much remained unknown and that it was uncertain if the idea of Thought-Particles would eventually have some impact or if it would fade away in a quiet death for a generation or two, if not forever.

They toasted each other with a glass of red wine and, for now, they would eat, drink and be merry. Whatever the fate of Thought-Particles, he loved Robin. That was not speculative.

"That's the nature of research, Roger," she said. "It can set the world on fire or be buried in an obscure graveyard. Don't let it burn or bury you."

"That's right, Robin. Uncertainty is a hazard of basic research."

As soon as Roger uttered these words, Ricardo appeared behind Robin with a sarcastic grin and sad eyes; he wore one orange sock, especially bright, and the other a clashing red, suggesting this was both a serious and a social visit. "Don't I know

212

it," he said. "Basic research gave me a quiet death in an obscure cemetery called jail."

Before Roger could respond – although what could he say? – and simultaneously with Ricardo's instantaneous disappearance, his smart phone dinged, signaling the arrival of an email. Curious as always, he glanced quickly at it.

"Who's it from?" Robin asked.

"Rabbi Magnum, whoever he is. I never heard of the guy. I wonder what he wants – a contribution? Who knows?"

"What does he say?"

"I'll check tomorrow. For now, let's have another glass of that mellow red wine."

In order not to disrupt his romantic dinner with Robin, Roger decided to wait until the morning to read the email, which pleased Robin.

Neither had any inkling of how Roger's world was about to change.

PART VI

RUDY

The Invitation

Roger read Rabbi Magnum's email the next morning:

Dear Dr. Resin,

I read in the New York Times the Op-Ed editorial by Nancy Weld on Thought-Particles. What an interesting new idea! A scientist in my congregation then alerted me to the negative letter of Anthony Lunt in Science magazine. I would love to know more about it directly from you, and I'm sure my congregation would too.

Since I'm not a scientist it's all above my head. To assure myself that I haven't let my enthusiasm run away, as I admit happens from time to time, I asked three scientists in my congregation (one physicist, one biologist and one physician), as well as a close colleague, Rabbi Manuel Sandinsky from Tampa, what they thought about Weld's article, Lunt's letter, and Thought-Particles in general. They found Thought-Particles intriguing with many implications, although the scientists thought that proof would be difficult to obtain. But the idea… that was quite something.

Rabbi Sandinsky was also impressed by Weld's article. I remember his exact words: "What a zinger of an idea, how relevant to religion, how substantive." He's a philosophical type and hard to please, so I value his opinion. I was particularly struck about his saying that Thought-Particles were relevant to religion, and I want to explore that further with him. He wasn't swayed by the scientists in my congregation who noted the lack of so-called proof. He has often told me that there's no such thing as proof without belief, but there's belief without proof.

Which brings me back to Rabbi Sandinsky's comment that Thought-Particles are relevant to religion. I'm confident you would agree that Judaism, as all religions, depends on belief. For me, personal 'truth' is sufficient for a meaningful life. In any case, I have no illusions that the broad topics of proof and belief are limited to one viewpoint. I believe your insight of Thought-Particles has the potential to influence and impact the Jewish community.

The observations you have made are remarkable and should not be ignored. Thus, I contacted a sociologist, Janeen Shepherd, inasmuch as sociologists have expressed some interest in Thought-Particles. She said that the political climate and economy greatly impact what's popular or ignored or vilified. That's why it's so important to note the date of creative works and to provide the context in which a creative contribution is made. For example, Vincent Van Gogh's paintings didn't sell in his era but are worth millions today. Why is that? The paintings haven't changed. I believe the world is ripe for Thought-Particles today. But I digress.

It is my honor, sir, to invite you to deliver a lecture about Thought-Particles to my congregation. If you accept, and I sincerely hope you will, please let me know the most convenient dates for you. I will make available whatever time suits you. That's how important I think your work is.

With my admiration,

Rabbi Rudolph Magnum

Beth El Hebrew Congregation

The Decision

"What do you think, Robin? A rabbi, no less. Hard to believe."

"I didn't expect that," Robin agreed, looking confused.

"Neither did I."

"It's ironic, isn't it?" she said. "I wonder what Rabbi Magnum would say if he knew you're an atheist and what you truly believe about religion. And he believes that Thought-Particles could impact Judaism? Wow! I assume that you won't accept this nonsense. No. Of course you won't. You won't accept his invitation, will you?"

As is no surprise, Ricardo made his grand entrance with such a question. He had a knack of sensing when things got interesting.

"Roger, Roger, Roger, don't be swayed too easily, either by Rabbi Magnum or by Robin," was Ricardo's initial reaction. "I realize that you may be receiving a powerful Thought-Particle from Robin that will make you decide what you do. If not, however, it's interesting to consider the contradictory points of view. Rabbi Magnum, no doubt a devotedly religious man, probably has intriguing ideas about Thought-Particles that never crossed your mind. Wouldn't you like to know what they are? Also, he obviously likes the Thought-Particles idea. Don't underestimate that.

"But then there's Robin, who worries about you and thinks you shouldn't get sucked into something you don't believe in through flattery. She's in your corner and doesn't want you to be exploited by anyone focused on their own agenda. She has a point.

"You may think that whether or not you accept to give a talk at the synagogue is a minor decision – inconsequential – no big deal. Don't be too quick. Bending one's values and commitments, making exceptions, can have more impact than you think and can reset the bar. As a scientist, are you satisfied without proof or at least compelling evidence – which, by the way, was my hesitation about you publishing your article – or would you be satisfied with belief instead of proof? Proof or belief? You've got a decision to make, Roger. Science or religion? Rabbi Magnum or Robin? How deeply committed are you to your values?"

Why make every small decision into a momentous crisis, thought Roger? Yet, what should he do? Proselytize Thought-Particles in a synagogue or stay on the straight and narrow path of science, rigor, and proof? This was ridiculous. It wasn't such a big deal. But...what was he after?

Robin felt his indecision and stayed silent to give him space. Ricardo looked directly into Roger's eyes, more curious about what Roger would decide than having an opinion himself or even caring what he should do.

Some decisions – not all – are neither right nor wrong, and Roger thought that this was one of those decisions. Flipping a coin would be as effective, maybe even more so, than looking for a rationale that didn't exist. The scientists were skeptical about Thought-Particles, but their opinions may change with more evidence. Rabbi Magnum seemed interested, but Roger didn't know why. Predictions are futile, no better than a toss of the dice, or heads or tails of a flipped coin. That's what life is all about sometimes. Not Thought-Particles or decisions, but about the unknown and happenstance. Roger wished that Ricardo could talk this over with Robin. Maybe they could come to a consensus. No. that would be a classic cop-out. He, Roger, would decide.

"So, what are you going to do?" Ricardo asked, getting impatient.

"Are you really going to accept, Roger? I get the feeling you might," said Robin, correctly sensing how Roger was leaning.

Robin was more intuitive than Ricardo, probably because she could think about Roger objectively, while Ricardo couldn't divorce himself from Roger, who was his alter ego as much as Ricardo was Roger's. Death didn't seem to change anything. Roger kept Ricardo as alive as himself.

Roger wondered what was wrong to get a religious point of view. Who would even know? Robin wouldn't suddenly change her mind about who he was. Being curious didn't mean bending values. It was a tornado in a teacup, a small decision that would change nothing in the long run. An analogy to virginity or sex was absurd. Anyway, as was Ricardo, Roger was totally partial to sex. Go for it!

Yet…Roger discussed this further with Robin, while Ricardo listened quietly in a corner of the room, keeping out of the conversation. Apparently, he planned on sticking around until Roger decided.

Robin remained convinced that Roger shouldn't accept. He had railed about the rigidity of religion so often and had complained how much religion fostered closed minds. He thought that religious observance was following a script instead of using one's own brain. And then, so many atrocities could be traced back to religion. It didn't make sense for him to deliver a lecture in a synagogue – or was it to be a sermon? If he wasn't true to himself, whom was he true to?

Ricardo and Robin had messed with Roger's mind.

"You're a scientist, Roger," Robin insisted, once again.

But Roger smelled adventure, another way to explore the unknown – and he was Jewish, ethnically speaking. That was written in his genes and had nothing to do about his thoughts on religion. Lots of Jews were more secular than religious. What Roger didn't know was that many Jews were abandoning Judaism and how that might affect his own life.

"You know what, Robin?" he said finally, "Maybe Nathan had it right. I'm able to prick my toe on a needle in the haystack! How in the world could I have reached the only group I never thought about? Weird, no?"

"You're nuts if you accept this invitation," Robin said, sticking to what she believed. "I bet Rabbi Magnum is flattering you to get a contribution, although I admit that he probably has some genuine interest as well. Anyway, you have such little knowledge of Judaism I'm afraid you will insult them without even realizing it."

"Perhaps. It's true that I'm never sure what to say until I start speaking and then I usually have too much to say! That's when I do get into trouble. And Judaism? Yes, that could be a problem."

Ricardo smiled, not because he found it amusing, but because it hit such a respondent note in him. He too seldom knew what to say until he spoke, and if anyone questioned his ideas, self-doubts crept in, and he often started saying things he didn't mean or fully understand. Agreement, however, emboldened him. His views tilted one way or another depending on their reception. His thoughts about jellyfish had started to waver when questioned during the trial. Maybe his interpretations were his imagination running amok. Maybe he insulted the jury with arrogance without realizing it. Ricardo wondered more than ever now, what would Roger decide?

Roger accepted the invitation. Robin rolled her eyes and chuckled.

"Okay," she said. "Better read a bit about the Torah before you go."

Now it was Roger's turn to roll his eyes.

And what did Ricardo say? Nothing. He did what he always did. He vanished without a word.

Roger's Lecture

Roger arrived at Beth El Hebrew Congregation a couple of hours before his talk to get a feel for the place and a chance to talk to Rabbi Magnum before his lecture. Partly because Robin had warned him that he would be out of his element in a religious community, and partly because his friend Nathan's synagogue was a strictly observant conservative temple also called Beth El, Roger assumed that Rabbi Magnum and the synagogue were conservative. The rabbi would be a conservative man with a serious demeanor in his sixties, wearing wrinkled pants and a sport jacket with a boring tie, and perhaps sneakers. He visualized a man of medium height, overweight, but not seriously, with a bushy gray beard and receding hairline, partially bald under his yarmulke, and in need of a barber to trim his hair colliding with his ears.

Where did all those biased opinions come from?

Roger couldn't have been more mistaken. Beth El Hebrew Congregation was a reform synagogue, bordering on reconstructionism, and Rabbi Magnum looked more like a salesman, or possibly a lawyer, than a rabbi, and nothing like Roger had imagined. He was solid, not pudgy, and very tall – maybe seven feet, or slightly less – reminding Roger of a professional basketball player in tip-top shape. Roger was just under six feet and too lazy to do much exercise. The rabbi had buck teeth that flashed a brilliant white when he smiled. He wore dark blue pressed slacks with a sharp crease down the legs, far from wrinkled. He had a crisp light blue sport jacket over a tan shirt buttoned at the neck, and a rust-colored bow tie sprinkled with ivory-colored dots. His black shoes were polished. He appeared to be in his mid-forties and was clean-shaven with a trimmed black mustache decorating his upper lip. His biceps bulged beneath his jacket, signaling that he spent considerable time in the gym lifting weights. Roger never would have guessed from his appearance that he was a rabbi.

Roger told the rabbi that his wife, Robin, was raised as an observant Jew, but he had little to no religious education; he never even had a Bar Mitzvah. His upbringing in the theater was not a good place to study the Torah. He stressed that his connection to Judaism was ethnic, not religious, and his message for the day – Thought-Particles – was scientific and had nothing to do with Judaism or religion.

In retrospect, Roger realized that his anti-religious bias was in some ways as incorrect as his expectation of what a rabbi would look like.

Worried about not being sufficiently versed in Judaism, as Robin had warned him, he told the rabbi about an experience when he gave a lecture at Hebrew University in Jerusalem. He had said that the Israeli audience would recognize scallops more easily on their dinner plate than they would looking at their remarkable eyes, which was the subject of his talk. He received boos and hisses after the remark: he had forgotten that scallops are not kosher!

Rabbi Magnum couldn't have been more understanding when they chit-chatted before the talk, and he listened to Roger with an open mind. When Roger said he was an atheist, the rabbi smiled benevolently and said, "No one can believe in what they don't fully understand. Good for you for admitting it. In any case, Judaism is always evolving. We must evolve with the times if we want Judaism to survive. Some of my congregants think I'm too progressive, and to some degree I understand what they mean. I think the congregants need to strengthen the bonds to each other and form a more integrated Jewish family. That way we won't let Judaism slip away. What do you think, Dr. Resin?"

"Makes sense," Roger answered, and he wondered how he fit into that family.

"Dr. Resin – may I call you Roger?"

"Certainly."

The rabbi reciprocated. "Please call me Rudy."

Rudy briefly told Roger of the thinking behind his decision to extend him an invitation.

"I thought that Thought-Particles provided a new way to bond Jews together, to keep the congregation as a closely knit Jewish family, like I'd mentioned. It's as simple as that," he said.

But it wasn't that simple; it never is. In fact, it wasn't simple at all. However, Roger had no way of knowing what Rabbi Magnum – now Rudy – had up his sleeve.

Rudy flexed his shoulder muscles, which seemed like a tic that made him look even taller than he was.

Roger nodded and said, "I see," when he didn't.

He had never considered Thought-Particles connected with God or religion. Maybe Robin was right: why did he accept this invitation? As informal and friendly as Rudy was, Roger became increasingly nervous for his lecture.

When lecture time arrived, the audience streamed in as family clots, glued together, some speaking continuously, others staring ahead without expression, as they filled the pews.

Hmmm, thought Roger, religion seems to be an effective way to trap an audience.

Rabbi Magnum had done his due diligence to introduce Roger. He had not only read about Roger's career, but he had also skimmed several of his science articles. He clearly didn't understand the science and called Thought-Particles genes (absurd) and proteins a type of DNA (even more absurd). Well, Roger thought, at least he tried.

Roger continued to worry that he would reveal his ignorance about Judaism, as Rudy had done about science. Was he about to make a fool of himself? No, not necessarily. It depended on the audience and environment, yet a wave of apprehension rolled over him. But then, Roger had to suppress laughing when he thought of how ignorant Rudy was of biology. Even school kids learn about DNA and genes.

"So," said Rudy finally, "with great pleasure, I introduce our guest speaker, Dr. Roger Resin, a famous scientist at the prestigious Vision Science Center, who is going to tell us about his recent insight on Thought-Particles. We are grateful to Dr. Resin for giving us some of his valuable time and knowledge. After the talk, please stay for a brief discussion. There's much to think about which reaches within and beyond our Jewish borders. Dr. Janeen Shepherd, a professor of sociology at American University, has kindly agreed to join us for the discussion."

Rabbi Magnum stepped aside, and Roger went to the lectern. He surveyed the array of faces in the audience – teenagers, their parents, assorted adults of various ages, and old guys, grandparents and other ancient survivors. He wondered what Rudy would see from his lofty height: perhaps a collection of yarmulkes on top of heads rather than faces. Roger took a sip of water that had been placed on the lectern and realized that he couldn't delay this any longer.

Just as he was ready to begin, his mind went blank, completely empty. Why didn't he write out his talk, or at least outline it? He had given so many lectures in his scientific career that he assumed there would be no problem. He was a pro.

But Robin had spooked him.

There was another reason for his sudden blank mind. This lecture was different. It was Jewish, so to speak. He was Jewish, but not entirely, not in a religious sense, and that had always been a conflict for him. Possibly that was why Robin had been so tentative about his accepting the invitation. He contributed to the Jewish Federation each year (they were persistent), many of his friends were Jewish, some observant, but he was embarrassingly ignorant about Judaism and didn't even observe the most common Jewish traditions. He had not attended synagogue in his youth, and after marriage went only on the High Holy Days. He felt as an outsider glowing with neon lights of discomfort when he was in a Jewish setting. How was he going to solve this blank mind problem?

By diving into the science, of course, as always. That would level the playing field. He didn't know Judaism, and they, presumably, didn't know science. If their knowledge of science was anything like Rudy's, he could tell them anything his imagination could dream up at the moment.

"Ladies and gentlemen, I'm honored to be here before you and tell you about my most recent work in science, specifically about Thought-Particles."

Suddenly, Roger soared. He was a scientist wherever he was – in a laboratory, at a cocktail party, even in a synagogue – and he set aside any thought of what the audience might be expecting of him. He would tell them what he knew and, most important, what he *believed*. That was as close to Judaism as he could get.

"Science can answer questions that have confused us for centuries, such as why do we look like our parents? Imagine, being able to solve such riddles," he said. "You can thank science for the answers. Science takes nothing for granted. It's all about observing with an open mind and testing for confirmation and clarification. Science has not only clarified our muddled, often erroneous, views, but has given us almost unlimited benefits that we take for granted, like mind-boggling electronics, long lives of good health due in part to antibiotics stolen from bacteria and other microorganisms, intricate, life-saving surgery techniques, and so much more, such as the ability to flip a switch and have light at night, and to find answers to questions by clicking a few keys on the keyboards of computers. You each have your own list of miracles derived from science. Especially remarkable, science has allowed us to sneak into our genes and repair even the smallest damage so that neither we, nor our children nor our children's children, will be plagued with disabling consequences of random, damaging mutations. An analogy would be finding a single, dying bush in the jungle in the midst of millions upon millions of trees and shrubs and vines and reviving it by sprinkling magic dust that falls specifically on the sick bush and not on any other plant or tree. These miracles were given to us by scientists asking the right questions and willing to devote their lives to answering them."

Roger, inspired, paused and scanned the audience. They were listening; he could tell. They were interested, and he continued. Roger was being Roger.

"Science has established facts and laws of nature, and these have empowered us to predict and improve outcomes to our advantage. But what about new frontiers and relevant questions that we don't even know exist yet? One of those areas, ladies and gentlemen, is the brain's miraculous ability to think and have judgment – both abstractions – that we attribute to our evolutionary success and main advantage over animals. However, animals think too, and have their own languages, which are foreign tongues to humans, so I believe that we will have to be humbler in the future as we learn more about the sophistication of animals. As for judgment and instinct, we're still in the dark about how that works in our brain. At this point, the best I can do is consider the brain as a whole – one extraordinary package – yours and mine and everyone else's brain."

Roger was firmly in his element now and told them about his studies leading to Thought-Particles. He covered the sudden switch in Diane's personality and summarized his observations of thought acquisitions in Virerium patients. He mentioned the thought exchanges between Vale, the plumber, and his wife, Gladys, and then, with a dose of humor, he told them about Juliette, his very own great-grandmother, and her amazing transformation.

"And how might all this be explained?" he asked, rhetorically. "Here's my theory: Thought-Particles.

"How we generate thoughts, how we transfer ideas and how this evolved to such a sophisticated level in humans, and I bet in many other species as well, are among the most important scientific, psychological and social questions we can ask. Answers, and there will be more than one, are still beyond the horizon, but the concept of Thought-Particles provides a new perspective to explore thought and, I submit, even what it means to be human."

Roger went on longer than necessary, which was not unusual for him once he got into his stream of thoughts rhythm.

The audience began to fidget and whisper to one another, and Rabbi Magnum started rearranging his yarmulke, fiddling with his tallit and checking his watch. Roger took the hints and told the audience that he would leave the implications of Thought-Particles to the following discussion.

He thanked everyone for their attention and then stepped aside after the applause, making room for Rudy to come to the lectern.

"Thank you, Dr. Resin, for an educational and thought-pro-voking (a few snickers could be heard in the audience) lecture. I invite you all to stay for questions and discussion."

Belief

Approximately twenty people stayed for the discussion, in-cluding the sociologist, Dr. Janeen Shepherd. Roger assumed the discussion would involve a lot about elementary science, such as what exactly are genes and how do they work, and are Thought-Particles connected in some way to genes?

But that's not what happened. Individuals in the group were more knowledgeable about science than the rabbi, but that hardly mattered. Rudy, who guided the discussion, didn't care at all – not a bit – about the science of Thought-Particles. It didn't even matter to him whether or not they really existed. He had recognized already when he invited Roger that proving the exis-tence of Thought-Particles would be almost impossible, as sci-entists from several disciplines had made clear, or at least would take more years to prove than he had to live, even though he was still in his 40s. Proof of Thought-Particles wasn't Rudy's concern.

He targeted the *weakness* of the concept – its reliance on belief rather than proof.

Rudy had watched his congregation shrink steadily. Although progressive, even for a reform rabbi, he suffered to see the Jewish family at large become increasingly secular. He assumed that was due partly to continual and increased assimilation and dispersion, as had occurred throughout the stormy history of Judaism. He believed science undermined religion in general. Effective medical treatments (for which he was grateful) had replaced prayer to treat disease, computer-driven networks and social media replaced the synagogue for extended relationships, and space exploration eliminated the heavens as God's residence and source of power. As the world evolved, God was being demoted, step by step. Although not against any of these advances, Rabbi Magnum believed Judaism needed a boost, if not salvation, and he wanted to do something about that. But what could he do?

Rudy imagined that belief in Thought-Particles could boost his congregation by providing an undercurrent that brought secular Jews back into the fold. He was willing to put older traditions aside, at least for the moment, to make room for the present with an eye toward the future. He was practical, willing to bend rules, experiment with ideas, and evolve with the times. That meant linking Judaism to science with belief. In his opinion, viability required progress, not repetition. He wondered whether Roger might bridge the past with the present to move ahead.

Rudy also had a self-serving goal. He figured that Thought-Particles could put a shining star on his legacy as the rabbi who restored Judaism. This ambition might have seemed wishful thinking, but Rudy believed in himself. When he spoke, people listened and heard what he wanted them to hear. And why not? His messages were positive, well-intentioned and targeted to the emotional core. He was convincing – a sincere rabbi cut from the finest cloth – with charisma, an essential ingredient to have influence.

As a scientist, Roger's mindset was to reduce mysteries to observable and testable facts, not to expand ignorance with beliefs; his world was intellectual and rational. But he sensed something different – something special – in the air, although he didn't know exactly what that was. He had no experience of religious fervor and was unaware – naïve – of how easily he could fall under Rabbi Magnum's spell.

Roger's life was about to change in a way that would surprise him as well as Ricardo and Robin.

"Thank you all for staying to discuss Dr. Resin's important insight of Thought-Particles, a discovery in the shadows about contagious thoughts disguised as substances," said the rabbi to start the discussion.

Insight. Discovery in the shadows. Thought-Particles. Disguised thoughts. How skillfully Rudy ignited the fire – a few words, an image, a hint of more to come. All with charisma, of course – charisma.

"Rabbi, I don't mean to be disrespectful, but Thought-Particles are hardly an important insight, or discovery 'in the shadows,' as you say. I would put them in the category of stretching the imagination, perhaps providing a catchy theme for a fantasy novel," said Walter, a shoe salesman, sitting in the front row. He read extensively – the Big Bang, lizards, whale behavior – just about anything about nature and science. He was a regular at the synagogue and a self-proclaimed "authority" on evolution, yet a creationist at heart. Some things defy explanation; religion fell into that category. So did Walter.

Roger sat still as a mummy, expressionless, listening to both Rudy and Walter. Thought-Particles were disguised fantasy? A discovery in the shadows? He was as skeptical as Walter.

"Thanks for the comment, Walter," said Rabbi Magnum, without emphasis of any kind, reducing him to background noise. "We may get to the philosophical question of what's a discovery later, time permitting. But first, I'd like to ask our sociologist guest, Dr. Shepherd, her opinion of Thought-Particles."

"Indeed," she said enthusiastically, at her chance to present her ideas. "Random thoughts going involuntarily from person to person! I wonder whose thoughts from the congregation I might be receiving at the moment without realizing it. That fits so well with my theory for the influx of people to urban areas, which I published a few years ago."

Roger had never heard of her work.

"People are drawn together by a magnetic force making them congregate, stick together," she continued. Dr. Resin has introduced Thought-Particles. I wonder if they might be the magnet attracting people together as well as the glue uniting them."

When Rudy heard this his smile radiated throughout the chapel.

"Thought-Particles might be an unconscious driving force for people to congregate in urban areas. Imagine, Thought-Particles creating nodes linking people into giant networks, resulting in the complex, interacting societies that we have."

Janeen Shepherd was in the zone.

Suddenly Ricardo was sitting next to Roger. "Did you hear that? Thought-Particles bringing people together into urban areas creating cities. Can you imagine how important that idea is, Roger? Ideas – opinions – just abstractions, the glue of humanity. Janeen thinks Though-Particles might explain the transformation of an agrarian culture to an urban culture. It's not just more jobs, or whatever. It's *Thought-Particles*!!!"

Roger didn't respond to Ricardo's enthusiasm. He liked the idea, but he was stunned, completely flummoxed. He didn't know what to say. Why hadn't he seen this obvious extension of his implications that he discussed with Nancy Weld? Why hadn't she thought of it? He had considered Thought-Particles as a force for anarchy, while she believed that they might be more a drive to democracy. Yes, democracy was closer to the truth. Nancy was right. But neither he nor she had taken that idea a step further. Even Ricardo missed the full implications.

Thought-Particles could be the driving force for social networks.

When Roger turned to acknowledge Ricardo, he wasn't there anymore. Roger looked around at the audience, but Ricardo wasn't anywhere in the chapel.

"My ideas weren't very popular then," Janeen went on. "I guess I was a few years ahead of what could be accepted. Thought-Particles may change the tide. Oh, how often even the obvious is obscure before people are prepared to recognize it. I suggested that there was a kind of unseen magnet that brought people together – that organized groups – into urbanized populations. It wasn't just technology or a quest for jobs. It was something else, something that was invisible, a pressure to connect with one another, a type of herd mentality, and then a glue that kept them together. The problem was that I didn't know what that magnet or glue might be. Now…Thought-Particles may be both…first the magnet and then the glue… the glue of humanity. This is so exciting!"

Roger was beyond himself. A sociologist recognized perhaps the most important implication of his discovery. Who would have predicted that it took a sociologist to understand the value of science? Strange indeed!

Civilization created by Thought-Particles – the glue of culture. What more could he ask for?

Several arms shot up for attention, which the rabbi ignored. He seemed anxious to get to his own ideas and dispense with everyone else as quickly as possible.

"Thank you, Janeen. Incredibly interesting. Do you have any more insights?"

"I love the concept of Thought-Particle networks," Janeen added. "How about…"

"But wouldn't any exchange of ideas do the same thing?" interrupted a voice from the congregants. "How do Thought-Particles differ from conversations and discussions?"

"No, No, No!" Janeen exclaimed. "Thoughts alone are not the same thing. A network created by random Thought-Particles happens without people realizing that it's happening. Am I correct, Dr. Resin? That's the important point, as I see it. Thought-Particles dominate by not being recognized."

"Yes, you are correct, Dr. Shepherd. Please continue. This is fascinating," said Roger. He was impressed how correctly she had grasped his concept.

She went on.

"Thought-Particles are invisible and random and contagious, like a viral infection. No one is communicating with anyone else on purpose, or even aware of it. There's no conversation or discussion going on. Does anyone convince anyone to be infected with a virus? Of course not. Thought-Particles can make people who don't think alike suddenly connect with each other, not because they finally agree on anything, which, face it, seldom happens, but because they infect each other with thoughts, like catching the flu, hopefully a good flu, a thoughtful flu. Sadly, that's not always the case. It could be an aggressive or evil flu. It's extraordinary. It makes me want to rethink everything. I always assumed there was a rationale – a purpose – for social movements. Thought-Particles change that notion. Things may happen by the spread of random particles. Pardon my French: *shit happens*. The shit is Thought-Particles."

Janeen, looking satisfied, sat back in her seat.

Roger thought of Diane's terrible headaches when she suffered through Virerium and cried, "*My brain is taking a shit!*"

Arms shot up again. Rudy couldn't continue to ignore everyone.

"Sue, what would you like to say? Enlighten us," said Rabbi Magnum to the prettiest woman in the audience.

Susan Plaget, a political activist who came occasionally to services, especially just before her daughter had a Bat Mitzvah.

"I would like to ask Dr. Resin if he thinks that Thought-Particles might have been responsible for the near dictatorship by our dangerous former president who called Virerium a hoax?"

"I don't think so, Sue. We were quarantined and social distanced to contain the deadly plague, as people have done for hundreds of years during a pandemic. People to people exchanges became virtual. Random physical infection couldn't take place. Government policy, politicians, the whole nine yards of our lives, became virtual, a cartoon, not in the flesh."

Sue pursued the dictatorship notion. "Do you think that under normal conditions Thought-Particles could lead to a malevolent dictator, a pandemic of political tyranny?"

Roger considered this question seriously. It touched on whether Thought-Particles could act as memes, his previous concern, for evil purposes.

"In general, Sue, I think one of the implications of Thought-Particles is that they favor social and political equilibrium," Roger said. "If diverse Thought-Particles are transferred randomly with a variety of overlapping ideas, I imagine that no one would dominate. I think that might keep civilization stable. For example, for every happy thought, there would be a sad thought. For every nomadic thought, there would be a home-maker thought. For every authoritarian thought, there would be a democratic thought. Diverse Thought-Particles exchanging among people would help the world stay neutral, relatively safe, at a stable low-energy level. In thermodynamic language, entropy would tend to increase in the population. I think the anarchy of thoughts might be the heart of democracy and lead to stability."

"You're stealing Nancy Weld's idea, Roger. Shouldn't you give her credit?" Ricardo said, suddenly next to him again.

"No, Ricardo. I said it was anarchy, she said it could be democracy. Now I think it's both, and neither of us had mentioned entropy," Roger whispered.

"Yeah, for good reason, Roger. Entropy is like describing a bird by its Latin name. Useless. Put the science jargon to rest if you want anyone to know what you're talking about."

Sue still wasn't satisfied. "But if Thought-Particles are like infectious viruses, and viruses cause pandemics, why couldn't Thought-Particles, which I gather are transferred through the air, cause a pandemic of one thought or another?"

"I can't say whether any given Thought-Particle can spread quickly through the population to cause a pandemic of any type. Maybe it can and would. I just know about individual cases. I don't know if or how a Thought-Particle replicates, or how fast it does, or how stable it might be. I don't know whether it's transferred in air or by contact of some sort, like Ebola or HIV, or by both air and contact. All I'm speculating is that thoughts can be particles that can be transferred from one person to another. There's so much more to learn. I'm opening the door, now we need to walk through it to explore the mystery on the other side."

This candid admission of ignorance silenced the group. Rabbi Magnum sensed this was the opportunity he was waiting for, the reason he had invited Roger. He straightened his glasses and looked in one penetrating glance at the audience.

"Let us not forget who we are, ladies and gentlemen – fellow Jews – and that we're in the Beth El Hebrew Congregation. What has been our history? Maintaining traditions and surviving persecution. But our congregation is dwindling, Jews are leaking from our core. The latest statistics show a shocking decrease in religious and increase in secular life all over the country. I ask myself whether Dr. Resin's Thought-Particles could help us stop the hemorrhaging. We must remember tradition, yes, but we also must think anew. We must move along with the times. I think Dr. Resin may have just given us a new tool that could help us do this. And Dr. Resin, along with Dr. Shepherd, have given us an inspiring idea that may…well…let me guide you through my thoughts."

"Are you trying to infect us with your Thought-Particles?" shouted Larry, the perennial jokester.

A few giggles made the rounds.

"No, Larry. Listen. I turn to the weight of the written word. Do you park your car where a sign says, 'No Parking'? No, you find another spot. If a passenger says it's okay to park there, but there isn't a sign that gives permission, would you be sure whether it was legal to park there? No. It would depend on what's written. You read articles, books, different documents to learn and get ideas. Hearsay is interesting, as is gossip, possibly correct, possibly rumor and innuendo, but always ambiguous, uncertain. Hearsay – spoken words – can't compete with written words on paper, and paper is a 'particle' carrying thoughts. What's written informs us, directs us, scares us, inspires us. We are a country of laws, but what does that mean? It means that the precise words that are written are what you can or cannot do, what's legal and what's illegal. It's the words that are written on something substantive. It used to be papyrus. Then it became paper. Today it's the computer. Aren't these all particles?

"I ask you, Dr. Resin, is a discovery even a discovery before it's published? Impact, credibility, discovery, are decided by publication, the written word. What if someone else – a competitor – independently discovers what you did in the laboratory and publishes it before you? Who is credited with the discovery?

You or your competitor? That's a conundrum: what should be and what is? You did it first, but you procrastinated, and your competitor published first. While history may level the playing field, the publication – the particle – of your competitor wins, at least initially."

Rabbi Magnum took a sip of water and scanned the audience, aware of his strong presence and admiration by his congregants. His expression showed how much he relished his power as his words were absorbed.

"Now I turn to religion, our world, the one we address here. The Dead Sea Scrolls provide what we know about Jewish history some two thousand years ago. If the information in those invaluable scrolls had been spoken words, they would have been lost, or if it had been miraculously preserved to some extent by word of mouth, their original meanings and credibility would have been distorted and unreliable. That's true for all history: what's written remains, even if it's not completely accurate. Descartes could have written, 'I write, therefore I inform.'

"Of course, these articles – particles – don't physically enter anyone's brain as particles, but they are examples of how information – thoughts – have weight when they are represented as particles of some sort.

"Let me extrapolate to art for another example. Consider Francisco Goya's anti-war prints and paintings, or Auguste Rodin's *The Thinker* sculpture. These works of art are a substance, which contain many thoughts which are transferred to those who see it. Aren't these masterpieces a type of Thought-Particle, like a written word? They don't preach; they expose in the form of a particle.

"And here's a remarkable fact. Thoughts and feelings projected from the art are given to individuals who look at the art. Let me repeat this important point differently. Sharing the meaning and impact of art – a conceptual Thought-Particle, as it were, containing latent thoughts and feelings – can bond people together into a single unit. Janeen just told us this in detail."

The intensity of Rudy's voice gradually increased and beads of sweat on his forehead reflected light as points of inspiration. He paused a moment. His eyes appeared to look through everyone, as if connected to an invisible power at the back of the room.

"We Jews are united by acceptance of the Ten Commandments and the Torah, which are also conceptual particles – and what particles they are – containing thoughts and beliefs. Oh, yes! Yes! The Ten Commandments, the Torah, the substance of our faith and beliefs, our history, our life. We must use the power of these particles to restore Judaism, to bring our family members back and unite them with the glue of Thought-Particles."

Chills went down Roger's back, his eyes moistened, he moved to the edge of his seat, leaving his body behind. He was all inspiration.

Yes, Thought-Particles, conceptually. He believed in them more than ever. The glue of humanity. Yes. The restoration of Judaism. *His* Thought-Particles. *HIS!* Rabbi Magnum's vision. Janeen's too. Oh, what company he had! The forces were coalescing. Power was being exercised. Everyone in the chapel felt this electricity. Roger was mesmerized.

Once again Ricardo appeared, this time standing and crying next to Rabbi Magnum. Crying! Tears were sliding down his cheeks. Tears of inspiration. Tears of a healing pool, a Jewish pool of Bethesda, a Sea of Galilee. Tears of the past and hope for the future.

How could Roger tell Robin about this moment? How could she, or anyone, understand the magic of the moment without being immersed in it? Words and explanations diminish some events, and this was one of them.

Tears now trickled down Roger's cheeks as well, and down the cheeks of most of those in the chapel, even Rabbi Magnum's.

Tears themselves were particles of shared thoughts and feelings, mirror neurons in action, separate congregants blending as one.

Rudy moved away from the lectern and paced back and forth at the edge of the audience. All eyes followed him – the powerful Rabbi Magnum – as if they would follow a tennis ball going back and forth across the net of reality. But it wasn't a game. Nothing like it. Was it even reality? It didn't matter at the moment.

Rabbi Magnum continued.

"Now consider this," he said. "God told Moses to come up Mount Sinai to receive the Ten Commandments, which He had written with His finger on tablets of stone. I emphasize *written on stone*. God told Moses to teach the Commandments. No one saw God write the Commandments, there is no proof of this story. Does that invalidate or lessen or devalue its deep meaning? No! I repeat, No, and again, No! It's all about *belief*. I repeat, *belief*. What power, *BELIEF!* Isn't that a concept too, like Thought-Particles?

"Is the body more significant than its invisible soul? I say again, No. The cliché 'seeing is believing' may hold some truth, but so does 'believing is a type of seeing.' Did the Virerium pandemic not exist because the pathogen wasn't seen? It existed, very much so, unfortunately. Has anyone *seen* Judaism? Of course not. Belief is not for human eyes. Neither is Judaism or tradition or a way of life. It's a *belief*, and that can't be proved.

"Dr. Resin – Roger – you have never seen a Thought-Particle. Does it matter? I don't think so. Do you believe they exist? I hope so. I'm sure you do. I do. The world must know about your belief. Do you hear me, Roger? Are you ready to save Judaism? I am, if you are."

Roger was beyond tears now, beyond words, beyond reason. He was aware of the sophistry and opportunism that Rudy was using so skillfully, yet he was in the palm of Rudy's hand and mind and religious fervor. Yes, he believed in Thought-Particles. It was like a vision. Where was Ricardo? He had to speak to him, confide in him, celebrate with him. But Ricardo was gone.

Rudy still continued.

"Thought-Particles, a brilliant blend of abstract thoughts and conceptual particles, a substance, like stone, believed to hold the written word of God that invades your mind. Thought-Particles, the power of belief without proof."

Someone in the audience stood up, crushing the magical aura. Rudy returned to planet Earth. So did Roger.

"Eloquently put, Rabbi. You have given us much to think about – words, art, God. But how do you see Dr. Resin's precise role in all this? Thought-Particles are interesting, for sure, but how do we benefit from them, as you implied?"

"A fine question, sir, and I thank you for it, because it introduces my next comments perfectly.

"Who better than Dr. Roger Resin, who gave us Thought-Particles, to reunite the secular Jews into our Jewish heritage? It will take work and effort, but I believe he can do it. With his Thought-Particles, which are Janeen's magnet and glue…you see…believe…that's what it's all about."

I can do what, thought Roger? He was shocked by Rabbi Magnum's hypnotic words, as if struck by a bomb.

Ricardo must have been shocked as well, since he popped up again, this time sitting next to Roger. He appeared worried, excited and confused.

"Roger, what's happening?" Ricardo asked. "Oh, my God, pardon the expression here, but are we dealing with a madman or a genius?"

Roger had never seen Ricardo so overwhelmed.

Before Roger had time to respond, which would have been difficult since he had no idea whether Rudy was insane or not, Rabbi Magnum turned to him, stood tall and rearranged his tallit and straightened his yarmulke, and did his shoulder flexing tic.

"Dr. Resin, Roger," he said, in a professorial manner, all hints of the visionary from outer space gone, "your major insight should not – must not – rest idly gathering dust. That Thought-Particles haven't been proved scientifically is to our – to your – advantage. It's a gift to exploit. Scientists will spend years scrutinizing the evidence with the standard cry of 'more research is needed.' And what will they say if someone identifies a chemical with properties that seem, by some clever twist of fate, to be a Thought-Particle? Please don't ask me what that evidence might be. Anyway, who would believe it? Maybe a few scientists, maybe not. Certainly not all. More years will be whittled away trying to strengthen or disprove the evidence. All good science, I'm sure.

"But a waste.

"Meanwhile, we, I at least, *believe* in the power of Thought-Particles, whether they are particulate or metaphorical hardly matters at this point. Identifying a Thought-Particle would probably reduce its strength. Reality can be less powerful than belief. Without tangible proof, Thought-Particles are free as a bird in the sky, which could make us soar as well.

"Spread Thought-Particles, I say, while scientists spin their wheels in the laboratory. Give inspiring lectures to our secular Jewish kin who have drifted away and bring them back into the fold by infecting them with the Thought-Particle of unity. Infect them with Judaism. I'll get you booked throughout the country to spread Thought-Particles in person and online. What irony to have science spilling over to become belief. Usually, it's the other way around."

Roger paled in disbelief when he heard this convoluted argument. Recruit Jews by infection with the concept of Thought-Particles? Does Rudy want me to tell secular Jews that they're infected with Judaism as if it were a disease, that they must return to their congregation as if it were a hospital? No. That can't be right. It's Rudy's poetic license making Thought-Particles genes of a sort, ethnic bonds. He's certainly no biologist, and that's not what I meant by Thought-Particles, but I see his point in this case. Maybe...I don't know...an interesting idea...

Ricardo whispered in Roger's ear, "You lucky bastard!! How do you do it? I told the prosecutor in my trial that I was a 'reverse scientist' – I created questions rather than solve problems, and I went to jail. You don't do your assignments in college, and you graduate with honors; you have tantrums, and you get rewarded; you tell nonscientists about your speculative Thought-Particles that you can't prove, and what happens? You become a prophet. You win by insults and shortcomings. It makes no sense. You are a 'reverse human being' – you make negative positive. Damn."

"Shhh, Ricardo. Rudy has something else to say. Quiet."

"I ask you, Roger, before the witnesses present here," Rabbi Magnum continued, "will you join us to put Thought-Particles to practical use to refill our coffers with the many secular Jews who have drifted away? And that, I believe, would only be the beginning. I see Thought-Particles becoming a universal weapon that spreads beyond our borders to link vaporous ideas to the wondrous findings of science."

"See what I mean, Roger? I'm out of here. You don't need me anymore."

And with that disgruntlement, Ricardo split the scene as seamlessly as he had entered it.

Was Rabbi Magnum a fake, an opportunist, a pompous ass, a clever devil, a savior? Perhaps none of these; perhaps all of them. There was no applause after Rudy's plea to Roger, just his few announcements of when the congregation would meet for the next event. Yet, everyone in the chapel realized that Roger Resin's Thought-Particles and Rabbi Magnum's vision and Janeen Shepherd's application to societies had joined forces to extend science to belief, to reverse the order of progress, to win by losing. It was one of those life-changing moments that can neither be forgotten nor repeated.

Ricardo appeared once again, this time in the audience, smiling with a thumbs-up approval. What a shifty guy! He seemed to have recovered from his bewilderment and winked at Roger. Their eyes met, and the two scientists, each straddling between reality and imagination, were locked together as one, as were Roger and Rabbi Magnum.

"Wow," Ricardo muttered at the very same instant that Roger said the same to himself.

Vaporous Ideas

Rarely does a single event determine destiny, but it does happen. Years ago, at the beginning of the 21st century, a young, relatively unknown Black politician – Barack Obama, a community organizer in Chicago – gave the keynote address at the Democratic National Convention. He said, "…there is not a liberal America and a conservative America, there is the United States of America." His charisma and vision of inclusion planted the seed to his becoming president of the United States four years later.

Roger launched his celebrity status by his stimulating lecture on Thought-Particles in Beth El Hebrew Congregation followed by the discussion and, especially, Rabbi Magnum's magnetism. Robin had advised him not to accept this speaking engagement, but he did accept and was ebullient when he returned home from the experience.

"Roger, I haven't seen you look this alive for a long time. Your talk with what's his name – Rabbi Mactun? – must have gone well."

"Rabbi Magnum. Rudolph Magnum."

"Yes, that's right, Magnum, sorry, like the champagne – certainly better than Mogen David wine."

"I love sweet wine," Roger said, but she knew that. "Anyway, you won't believe how interesting the day was. Rudy, that's what

Rabbi Magnum calls himself, went crazy about Thought-Particles. He wants me to promote them, at least the idea of them, the concept, to attract escaped secular Jews back into the fold. I certainly didn't expect that! Pretty ironic, wouldn't you say, an atheist scientist becoming a recruiter of Jews?"

Robin bit her lower lip, a habit connected with concern, and shook her head, ever so slightly, suggesting a tinge of disapproval.

"Am I hearing you correctly, Roger? Did you just say Rabbi Magnum – Rudy – wants you to recruit Jews to Beth El?"

Roger's face reddened, realizing how strange this must seem to Robin, who was raised as an observant Jew. After all his complaints about religion, and now this? He was a scientist, an unobservant Jewish scientist, an atheist. Yet, he was flattered by the offer, as well as embarrassed by it, so he blushed. With his crimson face, his silent language of color at the moment, he couldn't hide his discomfort.

It didn't matter. Robin knew that he was flattered, that he had considered the offer, that he might like to take it, but was too embarrassed to accept. He knew the absurdity of becoming a recruiter of Jews. Robin told him that it would be disingenuous and alienate him from the comfortable world of science he knew and believed in and loved. She could read him without words or Thought-Particles. There was no way Roger could fool Robin, nor did he want to. There also was no way he could escape from himself either, although sometimes – now – he would have liked to.

"Rudy stressed the importance of the written word," Roger said. "He considered thoughts written on a substrate as conceptual Thought-Particles, even though they don't get into your mind as a particle. He even called the Dead Sea Scrolls a type of Thought-Particles, and then, don't laugh, he also considered the stone tablet symbolically engraved with God's Ten Commandments as a Thought Particle."

It sounded less palatable when he said it to Robin than when he heard it from Rabbi Magnum in the synagogue.

"And...so what? I don't get it," Robin said.

"I admit, he stretched the Thought-Particle concept, which I meant to be an infectious agent, a floating thought that infects the mind. But his take on it affected me. Rudy is persuasive."

Roger looked away from Robin, searching to grasp why Rudy had affected him so much. He transported his mind back to the synagogue, where he heard Rudy's voice sing with inspiration that filled the chapel. How strange it felt to be inspired by a rabbi interpreting his insight of Thought-Particles.

"Listening to Rudy made me realize how important it was for me, personally, to have someone from the outside, a stranger, appreciate what I've done, appreciate me," Roger admitted, avoiding eye contact with Robin to hide his self-consciousness. "Do you understand? We are not our own judge; maybe our view of who we are is the least important judge. Our family and friends aren't our true judges either. And, as you know, I don't believe there's a God who judges me or anyone else. Rudy's judgment, or at least apparent judgment, was a revelation. My view of myself looking out differed so much from his view looking into me.

"I wonder how I would consider myself if I were a solitary creature with no one to judge me. Would I even have an identity in a vacuum? Am I who I think I am, or who others think I am, or who I think others think I am?

"I realized so much listening to Rudy," Roger continued. "We are not just ourselves. We are other people too. I am partly you and you are partly me. We don't know how many people we really are, and those 'others' who inhabit us change depending on the circumstances. Rudy and I were partly each other yesterday. It's amazing, Robin. We don't even own our experiences. We need to share them to become real and the people we share them with become partly us, and when they share their experiences with us, we become partly them. Our experiences and opinions and thoughts only become real when we don't own them entirely. And who are the so-called others? Those physically close enough to infect us and for us to infect them. We're back to Thought-Particles, at least conceptually."

As Roger said this to Robin, he wondered if it would mean as much to him if she wasn't there to hear it, to *really* hear it, as he sensed she did now. Its meaning to him was buried in its meaning to her. It was as he said it: they were partly each other.

"What else inspired you, Roger?"

He paused.

"I don't think it was inspiration as much as revelation," he answered. "Also, I envied Rudy."

"Envied? How so?"

He wasn't sure, but remembered Rudy scanning the audience, as if looking into the eyes of every person. Now he realized that he had it backwards – each congregant looked into Rudy's eyes. Oh, how much they respected him, and not because of his scholarship, or position, or sermons. It was because they knew that he respected them. He was partly all of them. It was Thought-Particles again, in a different light, not as substance, but as belief.

Yes, *belief,* the foundation of religion, the fabrication of God.

"I can't imagine Rudy inspired you, a scientist," Robin said, continuing to probe into Roger's mind.

"No. Nothing to do with science as I know it," Roger agreed. "Rudy was about as ignorant of science as a 3-year-old.

It was his *belief*, or willingness to use his belief, the polar opposite of science."

Roger felt his mind flood with a muddle of thoughts masquerading as if he understood what he was saying. He regretted thinking out loud. Why expose dirty laundry, such as impulsive thoughts and conflicted feelings? He had embarrassed himself numerous times airing thoughts that he didn't really mean or that were simply wrong. Well, so what? He could correct his errors. Wasn't what he gained by testing his ideas as, if not more, important than being right? Maybe. Not always.

"Roger, I think you think too much! Why torment yourself, why take yourself so seriously?"

Did he take himself that seriously? Of course. What could he say? That he shouldn't think or care? Rudy had recognized how serious he was and nurtured it.

Bingo! Roger suddenly understood; he didn't need Ricardo to help him.

"You know what really got to me in Rudy's talk, Robin? He made me understand what I never realized in quite the same way."

"Oh, Roger. You're talking in riddles again. Honestly, I try to follow you, but sometimes…"

"I know. Don't worry about it."

He told Robin about how Rudy, although making a mishmash of science, understood that the concept of infection by Thought-Particles would never achieve a consensus of proof. How could a speculative particle that transfers an abstract thought from one mind to another be proved? Rudy also knew, at least intuitively, that any isolated particle or molecule could be a contaminate – an experimental artifact – and wouldn't settle the issue. Prove that a particle is a thought?

Impossible.

Roger continued. "Rudy considered Thought-Particles a metaphor for belief, which he linked to a 'vaporous idea in wondrous science' to give them credibility. A bit much, I know, but…not so dumb. The phrase glowed in my mind. He didn't deny that Thought-Particles could be real, as I professed. But for Rudy, they were an idea generated by science turned religious! And that gave them the power of belief."

Could Roger, an atheist who knew nothing of religion, become a Jewish prophet? He looked around the room for Ricardo, who might give him a sign one way or another – thumbs up or thumbs down – but Ricardo wasn't there. He needed to figure out what to do by himself.

"Do you know what most impressed me, Robin?" Roger continued, "It was the need for belief and optimism in science, not only objective truth." He paused. "*There's no such thing as truth without belief,*" he said, with conviction. "That was a revelation for me. I've always focused strictly on the objectivity of science, the facts, the rigorous controls. Foremost in my mind was whether I'd made a mistake or whether my interpretation was too broad or too limited or just plain wrong – or wishful thinking. I created the most truthful narratives I could, given the facts that I had. But there are almost never enough facts for certainty or elimination of different perspectives. That's the soft spot of science, as well as its richness.

"Rudy made me see more clearly that belief and optimism infiltrate science and Thought-Particles. There are so many variables in science, some known, many not, in any experiment, in any thought, leaving wiggle room in the 'vaporous findings of science.' Belief is the balm allowing progress."

Roger was looking at the floor as he spoke, no longer looking for Ricardo. He paused for a moment and looked up at Robin. She was listening intently to him.

"Go on," she said.

"Rudy lives in the optimistic world of religious belief, and he made me think that the concept of Thought-Particles blended science with belief as an indispensable part of science."

Robin was silent. She wanted to support him, but she saw the world with a more matter-of-fact mindset. For her, science was restricted to tested facts with predictive value, not fantasy or belief. That was ironic, since he was the scientist, not she.

She broke the silence. "I get it, Roger. I understand the attraction of Rabbi Magnum, and also your conflict for what to do."

"What do you think that is?"

"Joining Rabbi Magnum means following everything you have always resisted – religion, 'soft' science. It makes you feel like a fraud, surrendering to commercialism and fear of what others may think, all unacceptable for the Ivory Tower of purity, for the world and values you admire. But that's not the only world, Roger. Haven't you said dozens of times that you regret only what you haven't done?"

Robin wisely stopped there. She had given him permission to outgrow Ricardo and be himself, to do what he never had done before, guilt-free.

Epilogue

Narratives in science or fiction don't have an obligatory destination. The story can always continue or twist to open new paths to explore. Any choice affects the journey one way or another. Not uncommonly, from a scientist's or artist's point of view, choosing the dramatic aspects – headlines, accolades, election to prestigious societies – often leads to footnotes in an accomplished life, while choosing the less visible, underlying aspects – silent epiphanies, resolution of torments, persistence – may lead to a more favorable destiny. Either way, happenstance generally has an unpredictable, guiding force.

Without Robin, whom he met by chance in front of an ice cream freezer at the market, and her love, a gift too dear to be bought, Roger would have been a different person with a different destiny. If there never had been the Virerium pandemic, or if Nancy Weld hadn't called him and published an editorial about Thought-Particles, he would not have met Rabbi Magnum – Rudy – a stranger who appeared from nowhere. If Roger hadn't accepted the invitation to speak at Beth El Hebrew Congregation, despite Robin's advice to decline, his legacy would have turned out differently.

Roger's destiny was a series of accidents, really.

Yet, happenstance cannot be attributed to chance alone. Roger sensed that the twins within him – the rigorous scientist who sought proof and the imaginative optimist who gave weight to belief – needed to couple, not conflict, to make him whole. And perhaps most important, he finally understood that what was accepted as truth could not be completely untangled from belief.

Roger accepted Rudy's offer to reach out into a world he didn't know, a world he had disparaged and avoided, to proselytize the concept of Thought-Particles. In doing so, he convinced multitudes of secular Jews to rejoin their congregations, not as observant Jews, but as members of the family.

A Selected Extract from One of Roger's Inspirational Talks:

...our precious Jewish family is hemorrhaging, and I propose that you allow previous infection by Thought-Particles to come to the rescue. Thought-Particle infection is silent and not by choice. Accept the likelihood that you have been infected by Jewish Thought-Particles in much the same way that you accept being infected with the flu. Denial doesn't work, and there is no known cure or vaccine for a Thought-Particle infection. Almost certainly Thought-Particles are integrated into your genes, by analogy with infection by retroviruses, which insert their genetic material into the host DNA and leave their mark permanently. Infection – Integration – Expression – Inheritance. Someday the details of each step of infection by Thought-Particles will be scientifically proved, but we don't have time to wait. The time is now.

You have no doubt been physically close to other Jews – your parents, close and extended family members, friends – making it almost certain that Jewish Thought-Particles enriched your environment and infected you. Consider that symptoms of infection of secular Jews are conflicts about rejoining your Jewish family in the synagogue or feeling as an outcast in expressive Jewish settings. If you had not been infected, you would not feel these conflicts.

I even propose that Jewish Thought-Particle infections contributed to the myth that Jews were the 'chosen ones,' a reasonable scientific explanation for what has been attributed to an abstract God.

So, I repeat, assume that you have been infected at some time with Jewish Thought-Particles, which would be more powerful than free will, just like genes are more powerful than wishes. Being secular is no reason for breaking away – being secular doesn't mean departure, it means adaption within your family. Accept your Thought-Particle infections and be who you are, a member of the Jewish family…

Rudy often accompanied Roger when he gave his lectures, and he often gave a short spiel in his charismatic manner after Roger had spoken. The two were a well-synchronized team. Many secular Jews returned to their congregation without feeling they had denied their skepticism of religion. There is no freedom of choice in infection. Rudy's congregation doubled in size in six months. Similar increases in other congregations were noted, and Roger became a household name as a savior of Judaism. Rudy shared in this distinction to some extent, as he should have, especially since Roger made it a point to credit him for recognizing the conceptual power of Thought-Particles.

Robin admitted she had made a mistake to allow her conflicts to interfere with Roger's decision to accept Rudy's invitation and then to join his efforts to recruit Jews back into the fold. She was grateful that Roger wasn't unduly influenced by her negativity, and that made her love him even more.

Roger didn't limit his talks to Judaism. He trotted around the globe speaking about the concept of Thought-Particles to audiences with diverse interests. Since Thought-Particles had not been identified yet, their power lay in their ability to stimulate research by the possibility of their existence, giving credence to the importance of *belief* and *optimism*.

Brief mention of a few positive results that can be attributed to Roger's lectures are warranted:

Philosophers explored the idea that belief can make abstractions real if their metaphorical power results in tangible progress. Religious organizations and politicians embraced this notion.

Physicists collaborated with psychologists and estimated that the probability of a thought transferal was roughly inversely proportional to the square of the distance between the donor and receiver, similar to the force of gravity. This stimulated research for the "thoughton," a hypothetical elementary particle. Although such an elementary particle hasn't been found yet, the possibility of a few sub-elementary Thought-Particles have cropped up. Their existence was implied if they combined with themselves or with other sub-elementary particles that were proposed. They were not considered candidates for true elementary particles until reassembled. Most exciting was the bold speculation that sub-elementary particles predicted another reality beneath (or above) the one in which humans exist. Daring scientists considered this possibility might signify a new universe, never seen before, dependent entirely on emergent properties.

This was mind-boggling flirtation with science fiction suggesting a new dimension of nature that could not be ignored.

Bioengineers adapted the concept of Thought-Particles to develop the ability of human brains to synchronize with each other wirelessly as well as with computers, and even with some animal brains. These were among Roger's pet ideas, and he was thrilled to see such projects succeed. A major discovery of human-animal brain linkages, based on the possible wave-particulate duality of Thought-Particles, was that dogs have abstract thoughts, such as appreciating the weather, having aesthetic values, and calculating how to get attention by more devious means than sniffing and licking and wagging their tails.

The most bizarre experiments of this type stimulated by the Thought-Particle concept were those designed to transfer thoughts from one species to another, such as a cat's thoughts transferred to a dog, or a cow's thoughts transferred to a horse. One scientist even conducted experiments to test whether a chicken's thoughts could be transferred to a snake. Not surprisingly, none of these worked. In fact, they were considered outlandish. However, both Roger and Ricardo believed strongly that these imaginative projects will seem perfectly reasonable in the future.

Already today, they point out, the Thought-Particle concept has promoted and advanced the potentially productive field of the evolution of thought.

Roger made several trips to the mangrove swamps of La Parguera in Puerto Rico, where Ricardo had collected jellyfish, to implicate Thought-Particles in Ricardo's speculations that jellyfish had a type of brain and visualized evolution. These trips were unsuccessful in furthering Ricardo's work. Roger concluded that science had not yet advanced sufficiently to appreciate Ricardo's speculations, which he felt confident were real and could still involve Thought-Particles. Ricardo went with him, of course. He was grateful for Roger's efforts and agreed to put these experiments aside until more progress was made on the evolution of thought.

Even more important than specific advances on various topics, the concept of Thought-Particles brought awareness to study sections that belief and optimism should be valid components of science grants and not a reason for automatic rejection.

This stimulated funding for projects considered longshots previously and put in the category of a nonfundable fishing-expedition – like Sam Leeman's sponge Slingshot protein had been. While that proposal failed to get the Golden Prize when Roger was a member of the award committee, Sam finally received the coveted award for his Slingshot protein, which ultimately provided the foundation for treating many neurological diseases, including ALS. This was one of Roger's great satisfactions.

Finally, speaking of prizes, a year before retirement Roger received an important recognition given by the president. When draping the medal around Roger's neck, she whispered in his ear, "I *Thought* it a *Particulate* honor to give you the first National Outstanding Imagination award to follow up on your earlier first Outstanding Scholar award at the Vision Science Center."

The president had decided to honor him with this national recognition after he blasted Congress with outrageous slurs and insults on television and other media outlets for not funding basic research to his satisfaction. He called the president's administration "lame beyond imagination," and continued his outburst saying that "the congressional morons have dropped their level to imbeciles and have the momentum to becoming idiots."

Long live Roger's temper tantrums! Where would he have been without them? No doubt without the awards he received or the respect he had won.

At a celebration party for the award, Robin toasted her famous husband, beaming while she said, "To my beloved husband Roger, the only person I know who can prick his toe on a needle in a haystack."

Nathan, among Roger's loyal friends and colleagues at the party, interrupted Robin's toast and said with pride, "I told you so!"

Rudy, still in extraordinary physical shape, went up to Roger and bent over – remember, he was almost seven feet tall – kissed him on the top of his now mostly bald head, and said, "I don't want to take any chances that my Thought-Particle of affection and admiration fails to infect you, so please accept my kiss as a heady experience.

And Ricardo? Where was he? Nowhere in sight. It was a different era, once again.

Acknowledgments

I am grateful to my many scientific friends and colleagues during my fifty-years in science, and to the National Institutes of Health, especially the National Eye Institute, for supporting my research throughout my career. Without the wealth of these experiences, I never could have created Ricardo Sztein in *Jellyfish Have Eyes* or his great-great-grandson, Roger Resin, in the present successor novel.

I am indebted to the The Writer's Center in Bethesda, where I took invaluable workshops by Kate Blackwell, Elizabeth Poliner, Robert (Bob) Bausch, Barbara Esstman, and William (Bill) O'Sullivan. These excellent authors, along with the other participants in the workshops, guided my transition from writing science for scientists to writing memoir, essays and fiction for the general reader.

Barbara Esstman, Lucy Chumbley and Dixie Barlow have given critical and incisive editorial comments, which have immensely improved the manuscript. I also thank Adele Siegal for her eagle eyes as a copy editor.

I thank Rabbi Roger E. Herst for reviewing the passages on Judaism, and Richard Drachman for sharing his extensive knowledge of physics with me, especially about the wave-particle duality, sadly two days before he passed away from a car accident.

I thank Margaret Dimond for her continual help in electronics and other matters.

I thank my publisher, Stevan V. Nikolic of Adelaide Books. His encouragement and acceptance of my writing has given me a platform as an author, which I greatly appreciate.

As always, I thank my wife, Lona, for her insightful comments and continued patience and love.

About the Author

After a 50-year career in research at the National Institutes of Health, Joram Piatigorsky devotes his time to writing. In addition to his many articles and publication of *Gene Sharing and Evolution* (Harvard University Press, 2007), he has published essays in *Perspectives in Biology and Medicine, Lived Experience,* and *Adelaide Literary Magazine*; a novel, *Jellyfish Have Eyes* (IP-Books, 2014; republished by Adelaide Books, 2020); a memoir, *The Speed of Dark* (Adelaide Books, 2018); two collections of short stories, *The Open Door and Other Tales of Love and Yearning* (Adelaide Books, 2019) and *Notes Going Underground* (Adelaide Books, 2020); and a collection of essays, *Truth and*

Fantasy (Adelaide Books, 2021). He is on the Board of Directors of The Writer's Center in Bethesda. His wife, Lona, and he have two sons and five grandchildren. His website is www.joramp. com, and he can be contacted at joram@joramp.com.

Made in the USA
Middletown, DE
13 December 2022

18269185R00161